U0127428

台北建成扶輪社贊助出版

Sponsored by

台北建成扶輪社
ROTARY CLUB TAIPAK KIANSENG

浮標
FLOATING BEACON

李敏勇 編集

Edited by Lee Min Yung

目錄

Contents

Chen Chien Wu

Pan Fan Ko

Chin Lian

Chao Tien Yi

非馬

白萩

李魁賢

岩上

William Marr

Pai Chiu

Lee Kuei Shien

Yen Shang

杜國清

許達然

曾貴海

李敏勇

Tu Kuo Ching

Hsu Ta Jan

Tseng Kuei Hai

Lee Min Yung

〈序〉

漂流，定置；瘖啞，發聲

李敏勇

　　台灣的特殊歷史構造，以1945年二次世界大戰結束為界，之前50年的日本殖民統治，以及之後國民黨中國的類殖民統治。因為台灣本土的民主運動，1996年起，人民經由直選總統而在某種意義上進入後殖民時代。但作為一個主權獨立國家，仍然因為憲法來自中國，而未臻完全，雖然台灣本土形成的政黨曾經在2000年贏得總統大選，且在2004年連任期間，曾致力宣示台灣與中國，一邊一國。

　　跨越日本與國民黨中國的政治歷程，反映在文化上的是從日本語到漢字中文的語言轉換歷史。其中，並隱含著國民黨據台統治初期的228事件──發生於1947年的反抗與血腥屠殺；以及1950年的白色恐怖──以反共為名，對付紅色異議份子的政治壓迫，一直到1987年才解除的戒嚴統治，曾長期宰制知識份子、文化人的心靈。

　　台灣的詩人在國度轉變、語言轉換的歷史，面對政治與文化困厄，詩史的描述和精神史的描述都面臨必須撥開表層，深入觀照的考驗。長期的國策文學驅使下，詩史和文學史一樣，有意義的探觸必須經由清洗歷史的污垢，才能窺見真貌。當下以台灣為名的詩史，經由詩選的採樣大多未能充分顯現台灣的真貌，常常受囿於在台灣的中國視野。

Preface
Floating, Positioning; being Mute, being Vocal

by Lee Min Yung

The modern history of Taiwan can be divided into before and after the end of World War II: Taiwan was Japan's colony for 50 years until 1945; afterward, the Kuomintang took control of the island in ways of colonization. Taiwan eventually entered the "post-colonial" era in 1996, when its citizens cast ballots to elect their president for the first time in history.

Yet under the current Constitution, envisioned to include all China, Taiwan has yet to become a sovereign country. The sovereignty of the country could not be considered complete, even if the locally grown opposition Democratic Progressive Party was established after the KMT ruled the country for four decades; even if the DPP won the presidential election in 2000 and 2004, and during its eight-year term the government made efforts to declare that Taiwan and China are two separate countries.

Paralleling the political change of 1945 was a cultural catastrophe. Taiwanese were forced to change overnight the language they used to express themselves from Japanese to Mandarin. An initial trauma was imprinted on all these—the February 28, 1947 Incident: the Chinese Nationalist army launched a bloody crackdown on civilian uprisings on the island of Formosa. The incident was followed by a white-terror period, in which the KMT continued in clamping down on all dissident in the name of anti-Communism. The threat of political persecutions, haunting the minds of Taiwan's writers and intellectuals, did not stop until after 1987 when the martial-law rule was lifted.

Against the background, the challenge confronting Taiwanese poets was twofold: political and cultural, affected by forced identity and language changes. The attempt to describe the history of Taiwanese poetry therefore must also address the two aspects.

A relevant and truthful investigation into Taiwan's history of poetry and literature requires discarding long-established interpretations created in the interest of the Chinese ruler and the consolidation of its power. Yet many contemporary anthologies of "Taiwanese" poetry failed to reveal Taiwan in its broad horizon due to slanted selections with perspectives often confined to a Chinese, rather than a Taiwanese, tradition.

　　《浮標》這本詩選，嘗試以台灣性、現代性為座標，兼顧藝術與社會的視野，純粹與參與的風格，選編「笠」——二十位詩人的詩，以漢英對照方式呈現台灣戰後詩的某種風貌。「笠」是戰後台灣現代詩傳統的兩個球根：「日治時代以日本語發展的現代詩傳統」以及「隨國民黨中國傳入的中國新詩運動傳統」之一，在戒戰長期化時代立基於本土，被統治權力的文化國策壓制，困厄中發展出來的聲音。

　　陳千武、杜潘芳格、錦連，屬於跨越日本語到漢字中文的一代，他們在二戰結束前以青年之姿尋覓詩歌之路，但隨即在政治變動、文化變遷中，經歷瘖啞的苦悶，仍然奮力發聲，為存在的實感留下見證。

　　幾百年來　從遙遠的彼岸駕船渡來此岸
　　就窺測不到彼岸的陋習
　　只有鄉愁——愛與恨交錯的惦念
　　受到彼岸的威脅　波蕩不安——疑心生暗鬼
　　NO，諾！台灣海峽　仍然一望無際……
　　　　　　　　　　　　　　　　——〈海峽〉　陳千武

　　春晨　我在睡醒的枕上輕輕撫摸嘴唇
　　撫摸著今天還沒有語言來找的嘴唇
　　　　　　　　　　　　　　　　——〈唇〉　杜潘芳格

This collection features 20 poets surrounding the *Li Poetry* magazine and is intended to present a view on Taiwanese postwar poetry. The standard of selection is based on the "Taiwanese-ness" as well as the contemporariness of a work, be it a piece of engagement or pure art.

Founded in 1964, the *Li Poetry* bimonthly has been dedicated to publishing poems that are relevant to Taiwan and of high aesthetic standard. The birth of *Li* was fruit of two traditions: that of modern poetry developed among native Taiwanese poets during the Japanese colonial period; and that of Chinese new poetry movement brought across from China with the mass immigration of the mainlanders to Taiwan after 1949. While the former tradition was being suppressed by the KMT ideologues, the *Li* poets tried to voice for Taiwan in their work.

In this book, representative *Li* poets are divided into the prewar, the intra-war, and the postwar generations of the 1940s and the 1950s. Chen Chien Wu, Pan Fan Ko and Chin Lian, born in the 1920s, were dubbed "the generation that crossed two languages." Power change forced them to abandon Japanese, in which they had begun to write poetry. They became speechless, but still struggled to write and to witness.

For several hundred years,
People have sailed across the strait to come here
Casting off undesirable customs.
Homesickness: affections intertwined with love and hate
And threat from the other shore,
  has engendered anxiety and suspicion
Well, the Strait of Taiwan still stretches to the horizon.

—— 'The Strait' by Chen Chien Wu

In the spring morning, I softly touch my lips on the pillow;
I touch my lips which are waiting for the worlds to come today.

—— 'Lips' by Pan Fan Ko

被綑綁得透不過氣的地殼
從深處的內部隨時要裂開
要迸出一股悲憤的岩漿

——〈沒有麻雀的風景〉　錦連

　　哀愁、苦悶、掙扎、追尋，從這一世代詩人的行句裡透露出
來。歷史的陰影，現實的陰影。儘管如此，詩人的隱忍叫喊中仍
然有光，有意義的光。

　　趙天儀、非馬、白萩、李魁賢、岩上、杜國清、許達然，都
是戰前出生，童年時代經歷太平洋戰爭，終戰後在轉換的國度成
長的戰中世代，處於歷史的接點的一代。但是背負著曾經被日本
殖民統治的歷史，在自己的土地上仍然不得不面對邊緣性處境。

倘若我是一顆石頭
沈入你的心底，怎麼沒有反應
倘若我是一句呼喚
震撼你的胸膛，怎麼沒有回音

——〈倘若〉　趙天儀

今夜凶險的海面
必有破爛的難民船
鬼魂般出現

——〈今夜凶險的海面〉　非馬

That from the deep, deep inside of the earth crust,
Which is so tightly bound up as to be unable even to breathe,
Something seems to be about to burst open and
   lava of indignation to spout out.

——'A Landscape without Sparrows' by Chin Lian

Sorrow, agony and struggling desire filled the poetry of the 1920s generation. Pressures and pains, however, did not deter the poets from conveying their massage in a meaningful way.

The intra-war generation, referring to those born in the late 1930s and early 1940s, includes Chao Ting Yi, William Marr, Pai Chiu, Lee Kuei Shien, Yen Shang, Tu Kuo Ching and Hsu Ta Jan. They began to write with the memory of the Japanese colonial rule not far behind them and the KMT government imposing identity change through education. They were also confronted with the situation of being marginalized on the land that was supposed to be their own.

If I am a stone sinking to the bottom of your heart
why is there no wave
If I am a cry pounding on your chest
why is there no echo

——'If' by Chao Ting Yi

on the treacherous night sea
a broken refugee boat appears
like a ghost

——'On the Treacherous Night Sea' by William Marr

半夜我被一聲巨響驚醒
天空高遠而星嘲笑
我是一點塵埃
在大地的懷裡仆倒地哭泣

——〈塵埃〉　白萩

堅持一直的信念
無手無袖
單足獨立我的本土
風來也不會舞踏搖擺

——〈檳榔樹〉　李魁賢

我總想知道
自己的宿命星在甚麼位置
有否閃爍燦然的光輝

——〈星的位置〉　岩上

詩人是齒輪間的砂礫
時時發出不快的噪音

——〈詩人〉　杜國清

冷，靜起的
火是熱情的聲音
燃燒，嚷成灰燼

——〈反調〉　許達然

At midnight I was awakened by a loud bang.
The sky was high and far, the stars laughing.
I, a speck of dust,
Fell prostrate in the arms of the earth, weeping.

———'Dust' by Pai Chiu

I stand on my firm beliefs
with my single foot on my land
I have neither hands nor sleeves
and will not dance or waver in the wind

———'The Betel Palm' by Lee Kuei Shien

I always want to know
The position of my astrological sign
Whether it glitters gloriously

———'The Position of the Astrological Sign' by Yen Shang

A poet is a grit between gears,
Often issuing an unpleasant noise.

———'A poet' by Tu Kuo Ching

Coldness will give rise to
The flames, a burning sound
Bursts into ashes.

———'Discordant Tunes' by Hsu Ta Jan

　　成長於戰後的這一世代台灣詩人，逐漸在發聲學上建構自己的位置，語言的出口沒有被堵塞的困頓。但面對的也是長期的戒嚴統治，民主發展不全症候的困擾。非馬、杜國清、許達然赴美留學後，留在太平洋彼岸的國度，在科學、文學和歷史學界存在，更以譯介歐美詩與詩論豐富台灣詩壇；而趙天儀在哲學，李魁賢在化工，各有進展，亦譯介外國詩歌；白萩比前行代台灣詩人更早在戰後漢字中文詩壇建立聲譽，詩藝出色；而岩上的素樸性，反映了本土的形色。

　　從困厄中立足，在這一世代台灣詩人的作品裡，有信念的堅持，有光輝的閃爍，有發出不快噪音的自覺、有釀成灰燼的燃燒之火，有石頭的呼喚，也有破爛難民船鬼魂般出現的驚覺，仆倒在大地懷裡的哭泣。

　　曾貴海、李敏勇、陳明台、鄭烱明、莫渝、江自得，是典型的戰後世代台灣詩人。出生於台灣的國度已經從被日本殖民統治轉換成國民黨中國類殖民統治時代，在漢字中文的語言情境中成長，也交集著台灣話語的生活況味。在「笠」的父母輩、兄姊輩傳承了本土與世界的詩傳統養分，但也更昂然地踏出腳步。

Unlike poets of the prewar generation who had to struggle with the sheer use of an unfamiliar language, the younger generation found a voice and position of their own relatively easily. Nevertheless, they were affected by the malaise arising from the longtime martial-law rule and later a raucous democracy.

William Marr, Tu Kuo Ching and Hsu Ta Jan went to the United States to pursue advanced studies in science, literature and history, respectively, after completing their undergraduate programs in Taiwan. They have since lived and worked in the U.S. The new continent offered them opportunities to appreciate European and American poetry. All three made efforts in introducing world poetry to Taiwan by translating into Chinese.

In Taiwan, philosophy-majored Chao Tien Yi and chemical engineering-specialized Lee Kuei Shien developed their own art of poetry, while also being diligent translators of English, Japan or German poetry.

Meanwhile, Pai Chiu was recognized by the world of modern Chinese poetry in Taiwan earlier than his Japanese-educated predecessors; and in Yen Shang, the simplicity in his language and theme reflects the true colors of the native.

In all, the images they use are striking personal metaphors that speak for the belief, concern and feeling of a poet in making independent voices.

Then came the postwar generation: Tseng Kuei Hai, Lee Min Yung, Chen Ming Tai, Cheng Chiung Ming, Mo Yu and Chiang Tzu The, all born in the second half of the 1940s.

The world they were brought into was Taiwan under the KMT's quasi-colonial rule. Mandarin was their language of learning at school; yet they were also fluent in Holo Taiwanese. For many decades, Holo Taiwanese, the mother tongue of the majority of local people, was banned in public sphere but prevailed in daily life; and the poets still got nurtured by the cultural knowledge and sentiments implied in the homey language.

Moreover, having been nourished by the efforts of the preceding two generations in writing and translating poetry, the postwar poets displayed self-assured creativity.

看不見人影

抖縮在屋角的

狗

無可選擇地

向四週深遠的幽暗

反擊

——〈荒村夜吠〉 曾貴海

從水平線透露的光照耀日昇之屋

福爾摩沙依然在海的懷抱裡

釀造夢想

地平線上

她的子民共同呼喚

台灣的名字

——〈在世紀之橋的禱詞〉 李敏勇

飄在風中茫然的打顫的旗幟

緊緊地握在死去的少年的手中的旗幟

——〈月〉 陳明台

這時，所有的希望

會化做一隻不死的鳥

——〈旅程〉 鄭烱明

Not a soul can be seen.
A shivering dog
huddles up at the corner of a house,
And attacks instinctively
the remote and profound darkness in all directions.

——'Barking at Night in a Deserted Village' by Tseng Kuei Hai

The light on the horizon shines on the house of the rising sun
Formosa remains in the sea's embrace
Brewing dreams
Above the horizon
Together, her people call out
Taiwan

——'A Prayer at the Bridge between the Centuries' by Lee Min Yung

The flag fluttering in the air and shuddering blankly
The flag held on tightly in the hand of a dead boy

——'The Moon' by Chen Ming Tai

At that juncture, all hopes
Will metamorphose into an immortal bird

——'A Journey' by Cheng Chiung Ming

清晨，拉開布幔
準備歡迎欣然的陽光

　　　　　　──〈凝窗的露水〉　莫渝

一種聲音
在內心不停地叫喊

　　　　　　──〈心臟移植〉　江自得

　　這一個世代的詩人更為積極地介入社會。曾貴海、江自得、
鄭烱明三位醫生詩人，在詩與醫療、詩與社會的多重領域實踐；
陳明台在學界，也為台灣與日本的詩交流努力；莫渝提供法國詩
的視野；李敏勇譯讀了世界詩，也積極參與社會改革，應許一個
更自由、美麗的國度。
　　更勇敢的發出台灣的聲音，更積極追尋真實國家的建構，意
志和感情流露在詩行，也顯示在行動。
　　陳鴻森、郭成義、陳坤崙、利玉芳是一九五○年代出生的詩
人，他們或早或晚在「笠」的園地登場，都執著於島嶼風土的根源
性。

流連中國海的魚群
倉皇奔竄，在那被劫掠的海峽
思索著「祖國」的意義

　　　　　　──〈漁父吟〉　陳鴻森

I drew up the curtains in the morning
to welcome the joyous sun

——'Dewdrops on Window Panes' by Mo Yu

I clearly hear
A voice
Crying out in my heart incessantly

——'Heart Transplant' by Chiang Tzu The

Most *Li* poets of the postwar generation are social activists. Tseng Keui Hai, Chiang Tzu The and Cheng Chiung Ming are doctors-poets, involving themselves not only with patients and poetry but also grassroots social and cultural movements.

They continued the endeavor of promoting exchanges of poetry from different cultures. Chen Ming Tai, a scholar, made efforts in introducing Japanese poetry to Taiwan and vice versa. Mo Yu is a prolific translator of French works. Lee Min Yung has been dedicated to translating and interpreting contemporary poetry in light of how his foreign counterparts deal with their respective societies and histories.

In general, the postwar poets voiced more assertively for Taiwan as an independent country, and they manifested their will and feeling in writing as well as in action.

Last, but not least, are the poets born in the 1950s: Chen Hung Sen, Kuo Cheng Yi, Chen Kun Lun and Lih Yu Fang. They joined *Li* at different stages of the magazine; yet all adhered to writing of and for the land they have been based on, with their distinctive tones:

Schools of fish lingering in to East China Sea
Disperse in a flurry in the looted strait
Pondering the meaning of "Fatherland"

——'A Fisherman's Chant' by Chen Hung Sen

在仰望雨露的花瓣上
我夜夜不休的織著
幾絲纖長而浪漫的夢
竟越來越深了

————〈雨夜花〉　郭成義

裝在壺中的水
被熊熊的烈火煮著
滾過來滾過去
想逃跑
四面是堅硬的鐵牆

————〈壺中水〉　陳坤崙

請用您靈犀的臂力
純熟的耕技
輕輕地牽動
繫在我鼻上的繮繩

————〈牛〉　利玉芳

　　更新的戰後世代台灣詩人,「笠」系譜裡更靈活、自由的一代。陳鴻森是一個經史研究學者,以古鑑今,以喻引喻;郭成義的新聞界生活體驗、世事閱歷,交織在詩裡的機智;陳坤崙既為出版人,亦為社會運動參與者,對微末事物的同情;利玉芳的女性思維,立足於大地的胸懷,延伸了歷史的國土,開拓了地理的視野。

　　以二十位台灣詩人作品形塑的詩情與詩想,詩意地呈現了一

On the petals that long for rain and dew,
I keep weaving night after night
some tenuous and amorous dreams
which turn out to be longer and deeper.

——'A Flower on a Rainy Night' by Kuo Cheng Yi

The pot is boiling
the water tries to escape
but all around there are iron walls

——'The Pot is Boiling' by Chen Kun Lun

Please use your dexterous strength
And mature farming skills
To lead and shake lightly
The veins on my nose.

——'Cows' by Lih Yu Fang

The four poets have been brighter and freer in dealing with their subjects than the former generations. A scholar of Chinese classics, Chen Hung Sen was keen on using allegories and make ironic references to present situations; In Kuo Cheng Yi, the experience of working as an editorial writer in local media outlets lent his poetry an insight into obvious matters.

A publisher and social activist, Chen Kun Lun expressed his sympathy for small things of the world; and Lih Yu Fang, with her particular perspective, explored the meaning of seemingly negligible lives for herself and for the country.

All in all, the poets in the book extend their thoughts and imagination to present the spiritual landscape of the Taiwanese. The island on the brim of the

個在太平洋西南海域飄搖的國度的心境與風景。這個仍然在尋覓著自己國家之路的島嶼國度，正從歷史的悲情暗夜走向光明的自由之路，像浮標一樣的島嶼正在為定置自己的國家努力著。

North Pacific Ocean seems to have been floating for centuries and in constant search for a name of its own. With the works of these poets, a path in the nighttime dark of the past seems to have gradually emerged to broader daylight. And like a floating beacon, the island of Taiwan is standing in the mists of history and politics while making efforts to secure a position of its own in the world.

(Trans: June Tsai)

陳千武
Chen Chien Wu
1922～

台灣南投人，現居台中市。本名陳武雄，另有筆名桓夫。
「笠」詩社發起人之一，為跨越日本語及漢字中文的詩人，
在台灣、日本、韓國的詩交流極有貢獻。曾任《笠》詩刊
主編，主持社務。
詩集《密林詩抄》、《不眠的眼》、《媽祖的纏足》、《安全
島》等十餘冊，並有小說集《獵女犯》，及翻譯日、韓詩選
多種。具強烈歷史意識及現實批評精神。

Chen Chien Wu (1922-) was born in Nantou. Using the pen
name Huan Fu, he began writing in Japanese. Chen was forced
to switch to Mandarin in postwar Taiwan under the Kuomintang
rule. He cofounded the *Li Poetry* society in 1964 and served as
editor-in-chief of the magazine. He has played a major role in
promoting exchanges among Taiwanese, Japanese and Korean
poets since the 1980s. He authored several books of poems,
including *Poems from the Jungle* (1964), *Sleepless Eyes* (1965)
and *The Traffic Island* (1965), a short story collection on the
Pacific War *Back and Surviving* (1984), and numerous volumes
of translations into Chinese of Japanese and Korean poetry. He
won the National Arts Award in literature in 2002.

我的血

我的
一半是父親的血
一半是母親的血

我的
妻，是陌生人
架著愛之橋永恆生活在一起
我的
孩子，有一半的我
另一半被陌生人擁有

我的
孫子，只剩下四分之一的我
四分之三是陌生人，和
另一個陌生人潛在裡面
因此，我只好緊握著妻的手
主張共享孫子的四分之二

我的
血，時而淡
時而濃，常向未知的神秘叫喊
可是由四分之一，又八分之一
繼續分裂了
終歸，連山的回聲也聽不見——

My Blood

Half of me is my father's blood
Half of me is my mother's blood

My wife, a stranger
Lives ever with me forming a bridge of love
My children
Have half of me
While the other half is owned by a stranger

My grandchildren
Have only one-fourth of me
And three-fourths of a stranger
With another stranger hidden inside
Therefore I cannot but hold my wife's hands
And suggest that we share two-fourths of our grandchildren

My blood
Sometimes thin
And sometimes thick, often cries to the unknown mystery
But keeps being divided into one-fourth, one-eighth and so on
Finally, it can hear no more an-echo off the hills

(Trans: K. C. Tu)

我凝視隨風起伏的草

草葉搖晃
我多情的心也搖晃

毫無秘密的我
深受色彩的映像
迷惑而頷首
我不知道色彩的影像
漩渦著怎樣的意圖……

怎樣的意圖？
怎樣的智慧和未來的夢？
我祇感覺沒有彩色的茅屋裡
封閉著閃閃的希望
我必須努力打開封閉著的窗
促進呼吸
讓希望延續下來

草葉搖晃
我多情的心卻不搖晃

I Gaze Grasses and Leaves Undulating in the Wind

Grasses and leaves sway;
My passionate heart also sways.

Completely without secret,
I am puzzled by the riot of colors and nod,
Unaware what intention
The riot of colors is whirlpooling

What intention?
What wisdom and future dreams?
I merely feel that the colorless hut
Is locked with bright hopes.
I should try to open the closed window
To ease breathing.
Let hopes persist.

Grasses and leaves sway;
Yet my passionate heart no longer sways.

(Trans: W. H. Hsu)

貝殼

妳死了變成貝殼
我會亂打沙灘的浪濤
每次湧來　潤濕妳
卻又不得不退潮
顯然　喪失了自我

愛沒有終局
愛加愛　愛到死
死不痛苦　不悲傷
死是貝殼　身歷浪濤的
邊緣　享受永恆
平靜底愛

A Sea Shell

You will become a sea shell when you die.
I will beat the beach's waves.
Every time they roll over to dabble you,
They have to roll back again.
Obviously they have lost themselves.

Love does not have an end.
Love increases love until death.
Death is neither pain nor sorrow.
Death is a sea shell braving waves'
Edges and enjoys eternal,
Peaceful love.

(Trans: W. H. Hsu)

海峽

海峽　屬於黑潮海流　不屬於人類的地盤
潮流穿梭在海底深層　悠暢……到冬至
季節一變　烏魚群就燙乘潮流　回娘家
帶來烏魚子當禮物　──幾千年來
海峽的規律　如此井然有秩序
自然構成的海峽　一望無際的海　屬於
水族們的自由天地
沒有國土分裂　不受任何統一的騷擾
幾百年來　從遙遠的彼岸駕船渡來此岸
就窺測不到彼岸的陋習
只有鄉愁──愛與恨交錯的惦念
受到彼岸的威脅　波蕩不安──疑心生暗鬼
NO，諾！台灣海峽　仍然一望無際……

The Strait

The strait belongs to the Kuroshio, not human space.
The sea currents shuttle back and forth
   at the very bottom unobstructedly until Winter Solstice
With the change of seasons, shoals of blackfish
   go home with the currents.
And afford fish roes as presents.
The strait has had its rhythm and order for thousands of years.
The nature-made strait with its broad expanse of sea
Constitutes the free world of aquatic animals,
Without separating the national territory
   or being troubled by unification.
For several hundred years,
People have sailed across the strait to come here
Casting off undesirable customs.
Homesickness: affections intertwined with love and hate
And threat from the other shore,
   has engendered anxiety and suspicion
Well, the Strait of Taiwan still stretches to the horizon.

(Trans: K. C. Tu)

愛河

愛　從偶然的機緣產生　在河邊
任那流水節錄的水銀燈一連苦澀地閃爍著
為何　他們稱讚這條為「愛河」？

愛河　漂盪著無人感知的悲寂
　愛　被隔在兩岸　伸手握不住妳溫暖的汗腺
愛河上　或需架設一座黃金的橋麼？
誰知道橋下搖晃著的是混濁的畸戀！

我忽而聽到一聲　港口　防波堤外
依稀地　拖著尾巴的汽笛
　自愛河翹拖著愛的拋曲線的別離

The River of Love

Love was called existence by chance on the riverside.
The mercury-vapour lamplights
   cut by the flowing water glisten acridly on and on.
Why do they acclaim it the Love River?

The Love River floats with people's unfelt grief.
Love is separated on the two banks.
People are unable to catch your warm sweat gland.
Doesn't the Love River need a golden bridge?
Who knows the river under the bridge quivers
   with turbid perverted love?

Beyond the harbor and breakwater.
I suddenly hear dimly
The song of the siren lingering
From the Love River that is drawing a curve of parting love.

(Trans: K. C. Tu)

杜潘芳格
Pan Fan Ko

1927～

台灣新竹人，現居中壢。為虔誠基督徒。跨越日本語及漢
字中文的詩人，亦用客語寫作。
詩集《慶壽》、《朝晴》、《青風蘭波》等，並有日本語詩
集。重視詩的精神性，並反省語言課題。

Pan Fan Ko (1927-) was born in Hsinchu. A Christian, she
began writing poetry in Japanese and was forced to learn
writing in Mandarin following Taiwan being taken over by the
Chinese Nationalists. She also writes poems in her native Hakka
language. Her poetry publications include Chinese-Japanese
Birthday Celebration (1977), Hakka-Chinese *Toward the Sunny*
(1990), two collections in Japanese and several books of poems
and prose in three languages. Her poetry tends to explore
spiritual questions and reflect upon the issue of language.

鋼鑽機

你我　住在旋迴的地球相反面
你是太陽我是月亮
正在同一時刻
現在　你的昨天是我的今天
在虛構的地表
只有穿過地核傳來的聲音才能確認互相的存在
長年習慣的假假真真的約定
現在　新的人腦穿孔開始了
旋迴的悲哀　順從者的正義成為鋼鑽機穿孔人腦
現在　仍然追尋太陽伴同月亮

Drilling Machine

You and I live on the opposite sides of the turning globe.

You are the sun and I am the moon,

Both living in te same moment.

Now your yesterday is my today.

On the fictitious surface of the earth,

Only the sound piercing through the earth's core

   can ascertain mutual existence,

Which has long been accustomed to the doubtful appointment.

Now new perforation of brain has begun

The sorrow of turning. The justice of the obedient people has become

   the present of the perforation of brain.

The search for the sun accompanied by the moon is still going on.

(Trans: W. H. Hsu)

唇

染上拂曉的顏色　嘴唇淡紅
以醒來的手指撫摸
柔軟而可愛的活著的嘴唇
人類唯一的嘴唇
敘述生涯長長體驗的唯一嘴唇
「住在污穢嘴唇的人民裡污穢的嘴唇的人，被燃
燒在天使的煤火燒了嘴唇 」
春晨　我在睡醒的枕上輕輕撫摸嘴唇
撫摸著今天還沒有語言來找的嘴唇

Lips

The lips tinted with dawn's light redness,
I touch with my awakened fingers.
The living lips so soft and lovely,
The mankind's only lips,
The sole lips narrating the long experience of the life,
"The people of the dirty lips living among the people of the dirty lips,
Their lips are burnt by the coal burning beside the angels."
In the spring morning, I softly touch my lips on the pillow;
I touch my lips which are waiting for the words to come today.

(Trans.: W. H. Hsu)

悲情之繭

一切生命，都會絞盡全力奔赴死！
向生命的彼端
人，
也不例外。

你和我，彼與此，甚至幼稚之軀，
瀕死時也絞盡一切，像春蠶吐盡其絲，
包裹自己在光亮的繭包裡。

跟隨一切生命的軌跡，
在不可計數的生命歷程之後，
如今，你我也正絞盡全力奔赴生命的彼端。

小小的蟲兒，細細的嫩草
樹木，花蕾，鳥兒…………
連吹拂浮雲的風也痛愛悲情之繭，
而將蔚藍的天空捲入白色的懷抱裡，
緊緊地擁著，用滋潤和藹的眼神和輕柔的語言，
加以擦拭使天空明亮。

The Net of Sorrow

All lives do their utmost to a dash to death,
The other shore of life.
Man
Is no exception.

You and I, here and there, even immature bodies,
Will endeavor like spring silkworms spinning out silk before death,
To wrap ourselves up in the translucent cocoons.

Follow the locus of life;
After innumerable journeys of life,
We now try our best to rush to the other side of life.

Small worms, tiny grass,
Trees, buds, birds,
Even clouds-stirring winds also dearly love the net of sorrow,
Embrace tightly;
With kind glances and soft language
Rub to make skies clear.

(Trans: W. H. Hsu)

非魚

很大很大的魚
在龐大龐大的海
大魚向天空噴出飛濺水柱
懸著七彩五色虹

厚大的魚背　揹著七彩五色的虹
幔幔浮上　忙忙的沉下
浮上　沉下　　浮上　沉下

「海中有龍門
　洪波頻頻騷動
　魚等渡過
　必成龍。　」

此處　遠離時空的此處
大魚揹負著七彩五色的虹
浮上　沉下　　浮上　沉下

燦爛　輝煌地太陽照耀著
此處。
非魚住的天・海
半圓形的虹　圍繞著它
與它同在　不論什麼時候

Non-fish

A huge huge fish in a vast, vast sea.
The huge fish shots out to the air
a splashing flying water pillar
on that hangs a rainbow with seven colors.

The huge and thick fish back
carries that rainbow of seven colors
Slowly, they arise
Quickly, they dive
Arise dive arise and dive

"In the sea there's a Gate of Dragon,
Where great ocean waves are constant,
When a fish manages to go through the Gate
It would become, for sure, a dragon."

Here, far away from the time and the distance
The huge fish carries the rainbow of seven colors
Arises dive arises and dives.

Splendidly the glorious sun's shining
Here
Where the non-fish lives
The sky and the sea
The semispherical rainbow

與它同行　不論到了哪裡
慢慢地浮上　忙忙的沉下
浮上　沉下　　浮上　沉下

surrounding it
Is with it, whenever
Goes with it. wherever
Slowly they arise,
Quickly they dive.
Arise dive arise and dive.

(Trans: W. H. Hsu)

復活祭

心在旅遊，以放浪的心情
身子不動，照常過著日子

從彼岸而來，
淡紫色的珍貴大輪蘭花，父親的贈品

復活！
是軀殼的再現嗎？
靈眼凝視對照之時

曾經活在歷史裡
祖先們的意識
無意識仍舊存在肉身現形的自己

不只是光，但願赤裸裸地奔跑
那豈只是他們而已？

語言是活生生的東西，
美麗的蘭花

Resurrection Offering

Unrestrained, my heat goes traveling.
While my body stays put, passing the days as usual.

From the other shore,
My father sends me a precious, large purple orchid.

Resurrection!
Does the body reappear?
When souls stare into one another's eyes.

The consciousness of my ancestors
Who once lived in history
Survives unconsciously in the flesh of my true self.

It's not just the light that wishes to streak
Doesn't everyone?

Language is a living thing,
A beautiful orchid.

(Trans: John J. S. Balcom & Huang)

錦連
Chin Lian
1928～

台灣彰化人，現居高雄。本名陳金連，在鐵路局的電報員生涯，使他具有鐵路詩人的稱呼。「笠」詩社發起人之一，為跨越日本語及漢字中文的詩人。

詩集《鄉愁》、《挖掘》、《守夜的壁虎》、《海的起源》等，並有翻譯多種。從現代性實驗到生活凝視，反映在他鍥而不捨的創作之路。

Chin Lian (1928-) is the pseudonym name of Chen Chin-lian. Born in Changhua, he now lives in Kaohsiung. Having worked until he retired as a telegraph operator for the Taiwan Railways Administration, he has been dubbed the railway poet. He belongs to the generation of Taiwanese poets who had to switch their language for creation from Japanese to Mandarin under political pressure. A *Li Poetry* founding member, he is author of several books of poems and translations. His major poetry collections include *Homesickness* (1956), *Excavation* (1986), *Origin of the Sea* (2003) and a Japanese book of poems *Fulcrum* (2003). His poetry ranges from modernist experimentation to realist description of life.

鐵橋下

彼此在私語著
多次挫折之後他們一直蹲著從未站起來
習慣於灰心和寂寞　他們
對於青苔的歷史祇是悄悄地竊語著

忍受著任何藐視　誘惑和厄運
在鐵橋下　他們
對於轟然怒吼著飛過的文明
以極度的矜持加以卑視

抗拒著強勁的音壓
在一夜之間　突然
匯集在一起
手牽手
哄笑　然後大踏步地勇往直前
夢想著或許有這麼一天而燃起希望之星火
河床的小石子們　他們
祇是那麼靜靜地吶喊著

Beneath the Steel Bridge

Muttering among themselves,
After so many frustrations, they,
  all alongcrouching, never once standing,
Accostomed to disillusion and loneliness, they,
Regarding green moss history, stealthily whisper.

Bearing all kinds of disdain, temptation and foul luck,
Beneath the steel bridge, they,
Regarding the angry roar of civilization flying past,
Give it their extreme pity and scorn.

Resisting the powerful decibels,
In the space of one night, suddenly
Gathering together,
Hand in hand,
They laugh, and then with great strides go forward,
Dreaming of a putative day when hope's star would burn.
Pebbles in the riverbed, they
Call out as quietly as that.

(Trans: Lynn Miles)

挖掘

許久　許久
在體內的血液裡我們尋找著祖先們的影子
白晝和夜　在我們畢竟是一個夜

對我們　他們的臉孔和體臭竟是如此的陌生
如今
這龜裂的生存底寂寥是我們唯一的實感

站在存在的河邊　我們仍執拗地挖掘著
一如我們的祖先　我們仍執拗地等待著
等待著發紅的角膜上
映出一絲火光的剎那

這麼久？　這麼久為什麼
我們還碰不到火
在燒卻的過程中要發出光芒的　那種火

這麼久？　這麼久為什麼
我們總是碰到水
在流失的過程中將腐爛一切的　那種水

晚秋的黃昏底虛像之前
固執於挖掘的我們的手戰慄著
面對這冷漠而陌生的世界
分裂又分裂的我們底存在是血斑斑的

Excavation

So long. So long
In the body's blood have we searched for the shadows
  of our ancestors
Day and night. For us, after all, it's been one night.

To us, their faces and body-stink are so strange.
And now
The desolation of this cracked existence is our one genuine feeling.

Standing alongside the river of existence,
  we're still doggedly digging
After the fashion of our forebears. We're still stubbornly standing by,
Awaiting the moment when the cornea, reddening,
  reflects the firelight thread.

This long? Why this long?
We still haven't bumped into fire,
In the process of burning up, emitting its radiance—that kind of fire.

This long? Why this long?
All we bump into is water.
In the process of runoff turning all to rotthat kind of water.

Before the false image of a late-autumn sunset,
Stubbornly excavating, hands a-tremble,

我們衹有挖掘
我們衹有執拗地挖掘
一如我們的祖先　不許流淚

Confronting the frigid, unfamiliar wodd,
Splitting asunder and splitting again,
  our existence all blood-splattered

We only have our digging.
We only have our stubborn excavating:
Just like our ancestors, shedding tears will not do

(Trans: Lynn Miles)

沒有麻雀的風景

鐵軌緊緊地綁住地球
高壓線爬滿了通至未來的路程
機車頭的集電弓發出裂帛的火花
啣命朝向未可知的方位奔馳的這頭怪獸
它們在監視　它們在威壓　它們在叱咤
整個風景似乎感知不吉祥的預感而哆嗦著

失落的樂園
已不再有麻雀回來了
少數偶而在熟識的電線上歇腳的也不敢久留
曾經成群的　一隻挨一隻鬧著玩的麻雀們
牠們也隱隱地感到
被綑綁得透不過氣的地殼
從深處的內部隨時要裂開
要迸出一股悲憤的岩漿

麻雀們還記得
有個風雨淋漓之夜
電線曾經拚命掙扎而悲戚地嘶鳴不已
但經過一陣虐待和蹂躪之後
鐵軌竟然沒有斷落　地球沒有被鬆綁

A Landscape without Sparrows

The rails bind up the earth tight,
The high pressure lines are strung along the
  road that leads to the future,
And, the pantograph of an electric locomotive
  shedding ripping sparks.
Those are on the look-out; those are coercing; those are commanding;
While all landscapes are shivering and trembling in awe,
As though feeling an ominous presentiment.

To the paradise lost
Never will the sparrows return again;
Once in a while a small number of sparrows take a rest
  on the wires familiar to them;
They won't stay for long, though.
Once sparrows played and sported shoulder
  against shoulder in great swarms;
They too are feeling faintly
That from the deep, deep inside of the earth crust,
Which is so tightly bound up as to be unable even to breathe,
Something seems to be about to burst open and
  lava of indignation to spout out.

The sparrows still do remember
That one night when the tempest was raging
  all the more furiously like mad,

如今每一根電線桿仍如一根根十字架
在被血紅的夕陽燒成一幅絕望的景象裡
在孕育著一縷期盼的一片平原裡
張開著雙臂
準備以殉道者的姿態接受烤刑

And the electric lines were writhing and
   wriggling desperately, keeping shrieking in agony.
Yet, unexpectedly, having been tormented and
   trampled upon for so long,
The rails were never cut to pieces as well as
   the earth was not loosened of its bond.

Yet now all the telegraph poles are outstretching
   both their hands as before.
Each pole standing after another like a cross
Taking the pose of a martyr about to be executed at the stake
Inside the landscape, which, having been charred
   by the blood-red setting sun.
Is now turned into one of depair,
Upon the vast expanse of plain that is still conceiving
   a gleam of hope.

(Trans: Lih Tokkiong)

游泳池

水裡　纖維質的密度極高

聲響　發自顏色與顏色的混亂

水裡　小孩的腳攪拌著

泅水者仍急促而喘息著
於漸缺氧氣的泥水中
泅水者仍急促而喘息著

Swimming Pool

The water is full of cellulose

Sound rises from the mixing of colors

Little feet stir rapidly in the water

And a swimmer gasps
In the oxygen-depleted muddy water
And a swimmer gasps

(Trans: William Marr)

趙天儀

Chao Tien Yi

1927 ～

台灣台中人，現居台北。台灣大學哲學研究所畢業後，在
台灣大學哲學系任教，並曾代理系主任，因政治迫害而離
職。後來在靜宜大學任教。「笠」詩社發起人之一，曾任
《笠》詩刊主編。
詩集《果園的造訪》、《大安溪畔》、《林間的水鄉》等，
並有兒童詩集多本，在兒童文學的推廣投入心力。

Chao Tien Yi (1936-) was born in Taichung. He studied
philosophy in National Taiwan University, and later taught at
the Department of Philosophy. While serving as acting director
of the department, he was forced to leave the university in 1974
due to a Kuomintang-conducted witch hunt that involved faculty
and students. Since 1991 he taught at Providence University in
Taichung. He now lives in Taipei. A *Li Poetry* founding member
and once editor-in-chief, he has published a dozen collections
of poetry, including *Visit to An Orchard* (1962), *By the Taan
Stream* (1965) and *A Water Village in the Woods* (1992), and
books of poems for children. He has made great efforts in
promoting literature for children.

倘若

在激流的岸邊
丟一顆石頭
在水上揚起一片浪花
捲起一圈圈的漣漪

在山谷的斜坡
喊一聲呼喚
在谷中激起一陣回響
敲起一句句的回音

倘若我是一顆石頭
沈入你的心底，怎麼沒有反應
倘若我是一句呼喚
震撼你的胸膛，怎麼沒有回音

If

On the shore of a river
I throw a stone
Creating a hole in the surface
and a sequence of ripples

On the slope of a hill
I make a cry
creating an echo in the valley
and a series of rolls

If I am a stone sinking to the bottom of your heart
why is there no wave
If I am a cry pounding on your chest
why is there no echo

(Trans: William Marr)

溶解與映照

你是一壺燒燙燙的開水
我是一叢焦綠的凍頂烏龍茶葉

你是一隻沒入蒼穹的鷺鷥
我是一片波光閃爍的冷冷的青潭

狂熱時，我溶解在你的水色裡
冷卻時，你映照在我墨綠的心鏡上

Dissolution and Reflection

You are a pot of boiling water
I am a pinch of scorched-green oolong tea

You are an egret fading into the sky
I am a cold lake with shivering wavelets

I dissolve my feverish self in your watery scene
and as I cool down, you leave your reflection
on the dark-green
mirror of my mind

(Trans: William Marr)

鳥的窩巢

鳥的窩巢
是用樹枝與草葉蓋成的原始建築
合乎美學的原理
是醞釀愛的溫床

鳥的窩巢
禁得起風雨的襲擊
烈日的輝曬
是哪一位頑童
來一個大搬家

那嗷嗷待哺的雛鳥呢
那展開翅膀護衛的母鳥呢
空了的窩巢
是劫後一片廢墟的焦土

窩巢搬了家
而愛的溫馨依然存在
不是任何暴力可以劫奪
叢林裡，重建的窩巢有曉暢的音符
青空中，愛的翅膀正在盤旋

A Bird's Nest

A bird's nest
Is an original architecture with twigs and grass,
In accordance with an aesthetic principle:
A love-breeding hotbed.

A bird's nest
Stands the attack of a raging storm
And the scorching rays of the sun,
But a naughty child
Steals and destroys it easily.

Where are the nestlings crying piteously for food?
Where is the mother bird to protect them with spread wings?
The empty nest
Is ruined by a sudden misfortune.

Although the nest is gone,
The warmth of love still remains
Beyond plunder by any violence.
In the grove, there is cheerful singing from
   a reconstructed nest, in the blue sky,
The wings of love are wheeling.

(Trans: K. C. Tu)

一隻狂飛的蜜蜂

一隻蜜蜂狂飛著
不知不覺地
飛進了玻璃窗與玻璃窗之間
窗外，那透明的青空世界
伴著灰暗的浮雲
而她在玻璃窗與玻璃窗之間
卻一直無法突破
飛出那小小的空間
她狂奔著，徬徨著、掙扎著
且逐漸地失去了原有的生氣蓬勃
當我悄悄地關起了玻璃窗
已逐漸地失去了鬥志的她
竟又昂然地
擺脫了一切
向青空世界騰空而去。

A Bee Flies Madly

A bee flies madly.
Unawares
She flies between the glass windows.
Outside of which is the transparent azure world.
Accompanied by the grey floating clouds.
And sandwiched between the windows,
She just cannot break through
And fly out of that tiny space.
She flaps wildly, struggles, and falters,
And gradually loses her endowed vigor.
When I quietly shut the windows
The bee who has been losing her will to struggle.
Is roused to high spirits
And frees herself from and bonds
To fly into the azure world.

(Trans: W. H. Hsu)

非馬
William Marr
1936～

原籍中國廣東，在台中出生，現居芝加哥。本名馬為華。
美國威斯康辛大學核工博士，為核能專家。
詩集《在風城》、《白馬集》、《非馬集》、《路》多冊，
翻譯多種，並曾編《台灣現代詩四十家》、《台灣現代詩
選》。移民美國，以漢學中文與英文創作，以現代知性呈
顯詩的世界，表現出科學家的詩性精神。

William Marr (1936-) was born in Taichung. Educated in
Taiwan, he moved to the United States in 1961. Having
received a Ph.D. degree in nuclear engineering from University
of Wisconsin-Madison, he worked as an energy specialist at
Argonne National Library until his retirement in 1996. Based
in Chicago, Marr has published a dozen books of poems in
Chinese, including *In the Wind City* (1975), *Collection of White
Horse* (1984), *Collection of Non-Horse* (1984) and *Road* (1986),
and in English *Autumn Window* (1995). He has also published
several books of translations and compiled anthologies of
Chinese and Taiwanese modern poetry. His mostly short poems
reflect a poet-scientist's pursuit of reason in art.

今夜凶險的海面

今夜凶險的海面
必有破爛的難民船
鬼魂般出現
在欲睡未睡的
眼皮上顛簸
向越來越窄小的
人類良知的港口
向一盞接一盞
滅熄了燈火的
腦門
死命划去

On the Treacherous Night Sea

on the treacherous night sea
a broken refugee boat appears
like a ghost
on the tired sleepless eyelids
jolting and rolling
toward the ever-narrowing harbour
of humanity
toward the land
where the lights die out
one after another

(Trans: William Marr)

人類自月球歸來

他想叫喊
水草纏著他的腿像群蛇
而失去重量的聲音卻遠遠
在太空艙裡
在模糊不清的電視上
浮昇

當時間在海面上砰然濺落
人類自月球歸來的消息
便適時地轟傳了開來

Man Returns from the Moon!

He wanted to cry
his legs got entangled with roads or snakes
his weightless voice was floating
in the spaceship
on the blurred TV screen

When finally the endless dream splashed down
on the ocean
A timely message was announced

MAN RETURNS FROM THE MOON!

(Trans: William Marr)

颱風季

每年這時候
我體內的女人
總要無緣無故
大吵大鬧幾場

而每次過後
我總聽到她
用極其溫存的
舌頭，咧咧
舔我滴血的
心

Typhoon Season

Every year at this time
the woman within me
rages violently
with no provocation

And when it's over
I always hear her
licking my bleeding heart
with her tender tongue

(Trans: William Marr)

日出日落

日出

畢竟

紅冬冬
掛在枝頭

為宇宙的事
煩惱得
是大得有點出奇

睡不著覺的
不祇我一個人

但滿懷興奮的樹
卻脹紅著臉堅持

看你的眼睛
這是他一天

也佈滿
結出的

紅絲
菓

日落

The Sun

Rising

The sleepless
worrying about the universe
wasn't me alone

Look at your eyes
they too
are bloodshot

Setting

a glowing red ball
hanging on the branches
it is indeed somewhat out of proportion

But the tree
flushed with excitement
insists
that it is his day's work
the fruit he
produces

(Trans: William Marr)

秋窗

進入中年的妻
這些日子
總愛站在窗前梳妝
有如它是一面鏡子

洗盡鉛華的臉
淡雲薄施
卻雍容大方
如鏡中
成熟的風景

Autumn Window

Now that she is middle-aged, my wife
likes to stand before the window
and comb her hair

Her only makeup a trace of cloud
the landscape of a graceful
poised maturity

(Trans: William Marr)

白萩
Pai Chiu
1937～

台灣台中人。少年時期即發表作品，參與過戰後台灣現代詩的許多詩社，「笠」詩社發起人之一。並曾任《笠》詩刊主編。
詩集《蛾之死》、《風的薔薇》、《天空》、《香頌》、《觀測意象》等，並有評論集《現代詩散論》。詩風演變和戰後台灣現代詩潮流相關密切，是被矚目的詩人。

Pai Chiu (1937-) was born in Taichung. He began to publish poems at the age of seventeen. Having participated in major modern poetry societies during the 1950s and 1960s, he co-established the *Li Poetry* and ever served as the editor-in-chief. His poetry publications include *Death of A Moth* (1959), *A Rose of Wind* (1972), *Symbols of the Sky* (1969), *Chansons* (1972, translated into English by William Marr) and *Observing Images* (1991). His oeuvre is closely linked to Taiwan's postwar literary development.

雁

我們仍然活著。仍然要飛行
在無邊際的天空
地平線長久在遠處退縮地引逗著我們
活著。不斷地追逐
感覺它已接近而抬眼還是那麼遠離

天空還是我們祖先飛過的天空。
廣大虛無如一句不變的叮嚀
我們還是如祖先的翅膀。鼓在風上
繼續著一個意志陷入一個不完的魘夢

在黑色的大地與
奧藍而沒有底部的天空之間
前途祇是一條地平線
逗引著我們
我們將緩緩地在追逐中死去，死去如
夕陽不知覺的冷去。仍然要飛行
繼續懸空在無際涯的中間孤獨如風中的一葉

而冷冷的雲翳
冷冷地注視著我們。

The Wild Geese

We still live on. We have to fly
On and on in the boundless sky.
The horizon forever withdrawing forever lures us on.
We live. We're always on the chase.
Feeling we're close only to see it's still out of reach.

The sky is still the sky our forefathers flew by,
Vast and void like a changeless advice.
We are the same wings as our forefathers', hard on the winds,
Holding to a will, falling in an endless nightmare.

Dim between the dark earth
And the sky, bottomless, deep, blue,
The horizon lies ahead
And lures us on.
We will slowly die in pursuit, we'll die
Like sunset's unknowing chill. We have to fly
Hanging across the boundlessness like lone leaves down the wind.

While clouds upon cold clouds,
How coldly they keep watch on us.

(Trans: Kwang Chung)

塵埃

疲困之後
一點塵埃逐漸掉下

冷漠的是那些高樓的軀體
冷漠的是那些窗口的眼睛
不甘心地
像蝴蝶在他們之間
起起落落

偶然歇在女人的衣襟
卻被嫌惡地彈下
偶然落在急行的鞋履
不被哀憐地踢掉
一點塵埃逐漸掉下
終於重重地摔向大地

半夜我被一聲巨響驚醒
天空高遠而星嘲笑
我是一點塵埃
在大地的懷裡仆倒地哭泣

Dust

Being exhausted.
A speck of dust gradually falls down.

Indifferent are those bodies of high-rise buildings.
Indifferent are those eyes of the windows.
Unwillingly.
Like a butterfly, rising and falling
Among them.

Occasionally resting on the front of a woman's dress.
It is hatefully flicked off.
Occasionally falling on a hurried shoe.
It is pitilessly kicked off.
A speck of dust gradually falls down.
And in the end drops heavily on the earth.

At midnight I was awakened by a loud bang.
The sky was high and far, the stars laughing.
I, a speck of dust,
Fell prostrate in the arms of the earth, weeping.

(Trans: K. C. Tu)

廣場

所有的群眾一哄而散了
　　　　回到床上
　　去擁護有體香的女人

而銅像猶在堅持他的主義
對著無人的廣場
振臂高呼

只有風
頑皮地踢著葉子嘻嘻哈哈
在擦拭那些足跡

Square

All the crowd disperses in a hubbub
To return to the bed
To embrace the scented female bodies.

The statue alone still clings to his ideology,
Raising his arms to shout
In the deserted square.

Only winds
Kick leaves all smiles mischievously
To wipe out those footprints.

(Trans: K. C. Tu)

無聲的壁虎

不經意地從詩中醒來
那滑音的殘餘
是密室中或飛或歇
一隻不寧的錦蛾

他的同伴已被驚嚇逃逸
祇剩他還在他的夢中飛翔

而那頭壁虎窺視已久
逐漸測好位置
在他幾度歇落之後
無聲而急速地撲上

我無端地哀痛了一聲
感覺已進入了現實的腹內

The Noiseless Gecko

Inadvertently awakening from a poem.
That lingering glissando
Is a restless little moth
Flying and stopping in a closed room.

Its companion, scared, has already fled.
Only it is still hovering in its dream.

The gecko has watched there for long.
And gradually determines a good position.
After the moth has stopped several times.
It noiselessly and rapidly makes an attack.

For no reason I wail with pain.
And the feeling has already entered the inside of reality.

(Trans: K. C. Tu)

雕刻的手

雕刻的手已經休息

在熄燈的工作室
冷冷的桌上凍結著一聲哀嘆：

一塊岩石已被囚禁
在一條魚的形象裡
成為裝飾

你驚覺地摸撫著滿身鱗刺
痛悔自己的生命
已死去的是始原的自由
而未來定型讓你潸潸哭泣

一滴眼淚掉在
魚眼上分外晶瑩

The Engraving Hands

The engraving hands are now at rest

In the darkened workshop
a sigh is frozen on the cold table:

a stone has been imprisoned
in the image of a fish
and become an ornament

you are startled at the touch of the scales
your life is in deep remorse
for the death of untamed freedom
and the future makes you cry

a tear drops onto the eye of the fish
making it shine brilliantly

(Trans: K. C. Tu)

有人

眾蟬鼓噪
而一蟬沉默
眾蟬沉默
而一蟬高吟

有人

對著天空深處
點叫自己
自己大聲的回應

Someone

all cicadas are singing
except one
all cicadas are silent
except one

someone

calls his own name
to the deep of the sky
resoundingly answers himelf

(Trans: William Marr)

露台

天空暗處留有幾聲雁聲
在死的內部蠕動了幾下掙扎

你站立露台，突出地球的一點
仔細地辨認所寄居的城市
聽鐘樓計數生命中卑污的一天

而夕陽終於無望地死在
暴齒凌亂的大廈之間

The Balcony

The twitter of the wild goose lingers in the dark sky.
Revealing its internal struggle against death.

You stand in the balcony, a protruding point of the globe
To observe circumspectly the city in which you reside
And listen to the bell tower counting this contemptible
   day of your life.

The setting sun desperately dies at last
Between the unruly high-rise buildings.

(Trans: K. C. Tu)

李魁賢
Lee Kuei Shien
1937～

台灣台北人。台北工專化工科畢業後，任職肥料公司工程師，後從事專利代理事務。
詩集《枇杷樹》、《赤裸的薔薇》、《輸血》、《永久的版圖》等，評論集多冊，翻譯外國詩人作品集多冊，尤以里爾克作品的譯介及歐洲經典詩人的譯介為重。植根於生活，探求人間性，重視現實經驗的藝術功用。

Lee Kuei Shien (1937-) was born in Taipei. Having received education in chemical engineering, he later worked as patent expert. He began to publish poems in the early 1950s. A poet, critic and translator, he served as president of the Taiwan Pen and of the National Culture and Arts Foundation. His publications of poetry include *A Loquat Tree* (1964), *A Naked Rose* (1976), *Blood Transfusion* (1986) and *Permanent Territory* (1990). He is appreciated as a translator of Rainer Maria Rilke as well as classic works by European poets. With subjects rooted in life experience, his poetry tries to explore the aesthetic possibility of the reality.

檳榔樹

跟長頸鹿一樣
想探索雲層裡的自由星球
拚命長高

堅持一直的信念
無手無袖
單足獨立我的本土
風來也不會舞蹈搖擺

愛就像我的身長
無人可以比擬
我固定不動的立場

要使他知道
我隨時在等待

我是厭倦遊牧生活的長頸鹿
立在天地之間
成為綠色的世紀化石
以累積的時間紋身
雕刻我一生
不朽的追求歷程和記錄

The Betel Palm

Like a giraffe
who wants to search for the free stars among the clouds
I strive to grow tall

I stand on my firm beliefs
with my single foot on my land
I have neither hands nor sleeves
and will not dance or waver in the wind

My height is my love
nobody can measure up
to my firm stand

I want him to know
that I am constantly waiting

I am a giraffe tired of a nomadic life
I will stand in the universe
and become a green fossil
with the accumulated tattoos of time
I will engrave the history
of my life-long search and struggle

(Trans: William Marr)

圍巾

圍巾是手的延長
纏繞在我的項際
脖子像伸出海面的潛水鏡
在寒風中破空前進
他的手纏繞在我項際
把體溫留給我身體

雲是圍巾的延長
飄動在山岳的項際
山在凝眸對視的流浪中
凝固成為日記上剪貼的紙花
他的圍巾飄動在我項際
把風姿留給我窗前

愛是雲的延長
醞釀在情人的項際
晚霞是時間壓縮的煙火
在空間呈現無限膨脹的浪漫
他的懷念醞釀在我項際
把名字留給我喃喃自語

The Scarf

The scarf that wraps round my neck
is an extension of his hand
my neck, like a periscope on the sea
moves forward breaking the cold wind
his hand, wrapping round my neck
gives me his warmth

The cloud that flutters about the mountain's neck
is an extension of the scarf
the roaming mountain, frozen under the loving stares
becomes a paper flower cut and pasted on my diary
his scarf, fluttering about my neck
leaves a graceful poise in front of my window

The love that flourishes amid the lover's necks
is an extension of the cloud
the evening cloud is a time-compressed fire
which fills the space with ever-expanding romantics
my neck is wrapped in the sweet memory
while my mouth mutters the name of love

(Trans: William Marr)

秋末的露台

大麗花
痴痴地開了一個下午
在秋末的露台上
披一身陽光
像刺蝟

脫掉了裝飾的綠葉
什麼都不是
就是乾乾脆脆的花

漸漸地
我也會脫掉花瓣
脫掉陽光
甘願為他開一生
在無人的
露台上

A Balcony in Late Autumn

A dahlia with sheer infatuation
has bloomed the whole afternoon
on the balcony in late autumn
with the sunlight radiating from its body
like the spines of a hedgehog.

Having cast off decorative green leaves,
it is nothing else
but a clear-cut flower.

Gradually
I will shed all the petals,
shed the sunlight,
and willingly bloom for him throughout my life
on the balcony
with nobody around.

(Trans: K. C. Tu)

幽蘭

像受傷的蝴蝶一般
離梗落在
手術檯上的蘭花
被百葉窗間隙落入的陽光
覆上囚衣的條紋

有如流行的瘟疫
蘭花紛紛落下
成為焦土中的部落
在等待著魂回故鄉前
一絲不自由的溫暖

我的愛也像
受傷的蝴蝶一般
享有一絲不自由的溫暖
在百葉窗帘的下面

A Secluded Orchid

Like a wounded butterfly,
fallen from the stem,
an orchid lies on the operating table,
covered with stripes of a prison uniform
as sunbeams filter through the blind.

Like a kind of spreading epidemic,
orchids fall pell-mell,
and become a tribe on the scorched earth,
waiting for a breath of restricted warmth,
before the souls return to their native homes.

My love, also like a wounded butterfly,
enjoys a breath of restricted warmth,
under the shade of a blind.

(Trans: K. C. Tu)

兩岸

愛的暗潮不自覺地
充滿我們不能跨越的距離

我們兩岸從同一個山嶺的起源
不自覺地各自奔赴前程
無形的水面蒙蔽我們河床一體的命運
距離常是變幻的風雲
即使有一天拉遠到看不見的異域
那種壯闊的汪洋仍展現愛的真實

距離相近會有激起波濤的顧慮
有攪動渾濁的怨嗟
但不論河面如何洶湧
愛是以底淵的深度衡量

我們的距離有不能跨越的神聖
不管是南岸風光，北岸蕭瑟
美的風景是和諧不是一致
愛的情意是深沉不是浮動

Two Banks of a River

The secret tide of love
fills our uncrossable gap

We both originate from the same mountain
but unknowingly each pursues his own goal
the unity of our fate is obscured by the water surface
and there is always the unpredictable distance between us
yet in spite of our divergence
we can still find love in the vast ocean

There is the worry of being too close
that the water might become torrential
yet no matter how turbulent it is on the surface
underneath there is the calm of love

The uncrossable distance between us is sacred
the south bank might be full of flowers
and the north bare
but harmony, not uniformity, forms such beauty
calm, not turbulence, is the true meaning of love

(Trans: William Marr)

雪天

我感覺那地層的胎動
當圍籠過來的烏雲愈積愈厚
開始有了雪花

嫩枝被寒冷壓彎了腰
忍不住就把重擔的雪
彈回風中四散

在愈冷的時候
才會感覺大理石的肌膚
有溫泉一樣的地熱

我要開花給無人看
結果在始終暖和的地層下
落花生一般

Snowday

I feel the quickening of the earth,
When dark clouds crowd around incessantly
And snowflakes begin to fall.

Tender branches weighed down with cold
Cannot help bouncing back the snow into the air
Scattering it in all directions.

Only when it is colder,
Can one feel the skin of marble
Warm like a spring
With the heat of the earth's interior.

I would like to bloom, showing no one,
And bear fruits under the ever warm layer
Like groundnuts.

(Trans: K. C. Tu)

野草

大地呀，擁抱妳的時候
感到全身痙攣的溫熱
有我的血，有我的汗
在底層躍動的生命
使我滿山遍野地歌唱
迎著陽光，歡呼明日的序幕

在荒野擁抱妳的身體
難道是宿命的存在嗎
我們常被阻絕在大路的兩旁
因為路上有轔轔的車輛輾過
有喧嚷的山羊成群拉出不消化的屎粒
有哭喪的哨吶對著虛空吹響

親切體驗在野地裡自由自在的擁抱
彼此依偎著溫熱的愛心
大地呀！我知道
妳不會計較在我的擁抱下隱藏身分
我們的宿命是唱出嘹亮的歌聲
歌聲才是我們存在的價值
愛才是我們存在的真諦

Weeds

O earth, when I embrace you
I feel warmth running through my body
carrying my blood and my sweat
the life that darts underground
makes me sing over the mountains and plains
I face the sun and salute tomorrow

Is it my fate
to embrace you in the wilderness?
often we are separated by the road
where wheels roll by
noisy goats drop their undigested excrement
and a flute cries against the emptiness

In the wilderness we freely embrace each other
we lean on each other's warm and loving heart
O earth, I know
you will not feel ashamed when I embrace you
it is our fate to sing loud and clear
singing is the only sign of our existence
love is the only real meaning of our existence

(Trans: William Marr)

岩上
Yen Shang
1938～

台灣嘉義人，現居南投。本名嚴振興，曾任中小學教師。
曾任《笠》詩刊主編，並創辦過「詩脈社」，發行《詩脈》
季刊。
詩集《激流》、《冬盡》、《台灣瓦》、《更換的年代》等，
評論集《詩的存在》、《詩的創發》。踏實的生活態度，對
自我的沉思與錘鍊，反映在作品中，留下心路的形跡。

Yen Shang (1938-) is the pen name of Yen Cheng-hsin. Born in
Chiayi, he is a retired school teacher and lives in Nantou. Beginning
to write poems in the 1950s, he co-founded a poets' group and
literary quarterly *Poetry Pulse* in 1976. Editor-in-chief of the *Li
Poetry* in 1996, he has published poetry, children's literature and
essays on poetry. His major books of poems include *Torrents*
(1972), *Winter's End* (1980), *Taiwan Tile* (1990) and *Changing
Times* (2000). His poems are reflections of his down-to-earth
attitude toward life.

星的位置

我總想知道
自己的宿命星在甚麼位置
有否閃爍燦然的光輝

因此每晚仰望天空
希冀找尋熟悉的臉龐
但是回答我的
都是陌生的眼光

直到有一天
我從流浪的路途回來
把一切的願望都丟棄
只剩一顆乾癟的頭顱
沒入深邃的古井
突然發現在那靜謐且清冷的水底
一顆孤獨的明星
輕輕地呼喚我的名字

The Position of the Astrological Sign

I always want to know
The position of my astrological sign
Whether it glitters gloriously

Thus I look up to the sky every night
Hoping to find the familiar face
But all those that answer me
are strangers

Until one day
I came back from the wondering journey
Giving up all my wishes
And all I had was the dry and withered skull
Sinking into the old well
Suddenly I discovered that under the motionless and cold water
A lonely star
Gentlely called my name

(Trans: William Marr)

陋屋

雨落在山巔
雨落在田野
雨落在溪底
雨落在道路
雨落在樹上
雨落在屋頂

雨落在棉被
雨落在
孩子（爸！這裡有水）
的嘴巴
雨落在黑夜

A Humble House

Rain drops on mountain peaks
rain drops on the fields
rain drops on the streams
rain drops on the roads
rain drops on the treetops
rain drops on the roofs

rain drops on the blanket
rain drops on
the mouth (Papa! water!)
of a child
rain drops on a dark night

(Trans: William Marr)

水牛

水牛總是埋怨自己灰黑的顏
非常嫉妒天空的藍
有一次無意間
水牛低下頭來喝水
才發現自己的角是刺向天空

天空是該殺的
然而天空高高在上
天空必也有俯身下來的時刻
於是水牛耐心的等待

天空終於垂下來了
在地平線上
水牛狠狠的衝刺上去
倒下然後朗朗地笑了
原來我體內也有這樣鮮紅的

Water Buffalo

A water buffalo complained constantly about his dark-grey skin
he envied the blueness of the sky
one day he lowered his head to drink at a pond
and accidentally discovered
that his horns were pointed at the sky

The sky must be killed, he thought
but the sky was up high
there must be a time, however, when it would come down
so the water buffalo waited patiently

At last the sky came down to drink
the water buffalo rushed toward the horizon
with all his might
and fell to the ground laughing heartily
my blood too is bright red

(Trans: William Marr)

杜國清
Tu Kuo Ching
1941～

台灣台中人，現居加州。美國史丹福大學取得博士學位
後，任教加州大學聖塔芭芭拉校區東亞系。並主持英文
《台灣文學研究》叢刊。《笠》詩刊發起人之一。
詩集《島與湖》、《雪崩》、《望月》、《情劫集》，翻譯
《艾略特文學評論集》，波特萊爾《惡之華》等多種，重視
驚訝、譏諷與哀愁的詩之三昧，呈現有情世界。

Tu Kuo Ching (1941-) was born in Taichung. A poet, critic
and scholar, he studied in Taiwan and Japan, and was awarded
a Ph.D. degree in Chinese literature from Stanford University
in 1974. He is now professor of the Department of East Asian
Languages and Cultural Studies at University of California,
Santa Barbara, and chairs the Center for Taiwan Studies. One of
the *Li Poetry* founding members, he is the co-editor of *Taiwan
Literature: English Translation Series*, published by the Forum
for the Study of World Literatures in Chinese at UCSB. He is
author of numerous books of poetry in Chinese and in English,
as well as translator of English, Japanese and French works. In
his theory, "surprise, sarcasm and sorrow" are secrets to good
poetry.

詩人

社會是製造歷史的機器
每一階層　一組齒輪
每一齒輪　一個生命
由時間的巨帶轉動
而那操縱的手　背後
仍有操縱的手　背後
是一隻看不見的手

詩人是齒輪間的砂礫
時時發出不快的噪音

大齒輪咬住小齒輪
小齒輪咬住更小的齒輪
繞著世代相承的軸心
共為理想的未來　轉動
而那看不見的手啊一招一揮
竟有一群　有齒無唇的微笑隱現
竟有一把匕首　於中午
刺死老嫗　又刺入
幼女的心臟……
神啊　您是唯一目擊的證人

詩人是齒輪間的砂礫
時時發出不快的噪音

A Poet

Society is a history-producing machine:
Every class, a gear,
Every gear, a life,
Driven by the eternal belt of time.
And yet behind the manipulating hand,
There is a manipulating hand,
And behind it, there is an invisible hand.

A poet is a grit between gears,
Often issuing an unpleasant noise.

A big gear into a small gear,
A small gear bites into a smaller gear.
Around the axis passed on from generation to generation
They revolve for the future of their ideal.
And yet at one beckoning or wave of the invisible hand,
There appears a pack of smiles with teeth but without lips,
There is a dagger, at noon.
Stabbing to death an old woman, and stabbing into
The heart of her granddaughter...
O god, you were the only eye-witness.

A poet is a grit between gears,
Often issuing an unpleasant noise.

有的齒輪　失落
有的齒輪　腐敗
有的齒輪　謀叛
有的齒輪　金光閃閃
而大多數　似乎已看見那不見的手
卻仍安分守己　保持沉默

詩人是齒輪間的砂礫
時時發出不快的噪音

齒輪　無血　卻有過剩的潤滑油
齒輪　有聲　卻無表達感情的語言
齒輪　切切　咬住鄉土的苦悶
齒輪　遲遲　軋出曖昧的喜怒
齒輪　急急　輾示時代的軌跡
時代的證詞　發自
齒輪間的砂礫：
詩人不昧的良心
每當自我刑求
發出不快的噪音

Some gears lost,

Some gears corrupt,

Some gears plotting a rebellion,

Some gears shining with gold.

But the majority seem to have seen the invisible hand,

And yet abide by the law and keep silent.

A poet is a grit between gears,

Often issuing an unpleasant noise.

Some gears have no blood but excessive lubricating grease;

Some gears have voices but no words to express their feelings,

Some gears gnash their teeth in an agony for native land

Some gears gradually click out ambiguous joys and angers,

Some gears hastily roll to reveal the path of the times.

The testimony of the times

Blasts from the grit between gears:

A poet's sheer conscience,

Whenever self-tortured,

Issues an unpleasant noise.

(Trans: K. C. Tu)

月光

月亮
陰溝的出口
在天國岸邊
傾瀉著
乳香的榮光

夜
一片
汪洋

此岸的世界
氾濫著月光
女神的洗澡水

Moonlight

The moon,
An outlet of the sewer,
On the shore of Heaven,
Pouring down
A milky glory.

The night,
A vast expanse
Of water.

The world on this shore
Is deluged with moonlight.
The bath water of goddesses.

(Trans: K. C. Tu)

懷鄉石

暴風雨後
洪水沖毀了祖田
一顆石頭千翻萬滾
遠離了家園

失落　在路邊
蒙塵的玫瑰窗下
任西風　吹掠

萬水千山　滾過
一顆殘岩　傷痕累累
西方日落　驀然回首
洋燈　閃亮在
傳統的巷尾

一顆頑石　遠離家園
擱淺在異國的斜坡
那冥頑的土質　永遠
飽含鄉土磁性
感應著　鄉情
千里盈盈

故鄉　永恆的磁礦
在遊子心盤上
思念的指針
動盪之後　永遠
定向故鄉

Homesick Rock

After the storm,
Floods dashed away the ancestral field.
A rock tossed and tumbled,
Was carried away from home.

Lost by the roadside,
Under the dusty rose windows,
Swept and plundered by the west wind.

Rolling over ten thousand crags and torrents,
The rock survives with countless bruises.
The sun sets in the west,
Turning round suddenly:
A foreign lamp is flashing
At the tail end of a traditional lane.

The stubborn rock, far away from its homeland,
Runs aground at a slope of a foreign country.
The uncompliant nature of its soil always
Fully contains the magnetic of the native land.
And inducts nostalgia
Brimming over a thousand miles.

The native land is an eternal lodestone:
In the compass of a wanderer's heart,
The indicator of longing,
After turbulence, always
Steadily points to the native land.

(Trans: K. C. Tu)

酒歌

1

我以酒杯
嘗盡了人生的滋味
不知誰是我最後的女人

妳的臉影　多嫵媚
浮映在這澄紅的杯間
今夜　為妳乾杯
讓我把妳吞進我的心
讓妳在我心上　盛開　美艷
薄命的妳呀　從此不再歡怨
妳是我真正最後的女人

2

我的眼淚
滴盡了人生的滋味
不知我是誰最後的女人

你的臉影　多憔悴
浮映在這澄紅的杯間
今夜　為你乾杯
讓我把你吞進我的心
讓你在我心上　溫存　沉湎
薄倖的你呀　但願不再負心
我是你真正最後的女人

Drinking Songs

1

Cup after cup
I have fasted all flavors of life,
and wonder who will be my last woman.

Your face lovely and charming
reflects and floats in this pink glass
Tonight to drink a toast to you,
let me swallow you into my heart,
let your beauty fully bloom in my heart.
You will lament no more your ill luck
you are really my last woman.

2

Drop after drop
I have tasted all tears of life,
and wonder whose last woman I will be.

Your face worn and worried
reflects and floats in this pink glass.
Tonight to drink a toast to you,
let me swallow you into my heart,
let you swim in the tender love of my heart.
You will not be a drifter any more
I am really your last woman.

(Trans: K. C. Tu)

許達然
Hsu Ta Jan
1940 ～

台灣台南人，現居芝加哥。本名許文雄，在台灣東海大學、哈佛大學、芝加哥大學修習歷史並獲博士學位。現為美國西北大學歷史系，亞非研究系及比較文學榮譽教授，東海大學歷史所講座教授，亦為傑出散文家。

詩集《違章建築》等，散文集《遠方》、《土》、《吐》、《風情的理解》多種，重視漢字的肌理特色與豐富涵義，在語言的斷與連有飛躍的表現，探觸現實，富人道精神。

Hsu Ta Jan (1940-) is the pen name of Hsu Wen-hsiung, essayist, poet and scholar. Born in Tainan, he majored in history in Taiwan and pursued advanced studies in the United States. He received a Ph.D. degree from University of Chicago, and is professor emeritus of Northwestern University. He has taught in Taiwan's Tunghai University since 2007. His major literary works include a poetry collection *Squatter* (1986), and essay collections *A Distant Place* (1965), *Soil* (1979), *Spew* (1984) and *Sympathetic Understanding* (1991). His poetry is noted for the use of puns and junctions of disparate words to highlight human conditions.

路

阿祖的兩輪前是阿公　拖載日本仔
拖不掉侮辱　倒在血池

阿公的兩輪後是阿媽　推賣熱甘藷
推不離艱苦　倒在半路

阿爸的三輪上是阿爸　趕忙敢忙
踏不出希望　倒在街上

別人的四輪上是我啦　敢快趕快
駛不開驚險　活爭時間

The Road

Before great-grandpa's two wheels was grandpa,
   pulling to carry Japanese;
Unable to pull out of snub, he collapsed in his own blood.

Behind grandpa's two wheels was grandma,
   pushing to peddle hot sweet potatoes;
Unable to push away misery, she collapsed on the street.

On dad's own three wheels was dad himself, pedaling frantically;
Unable to pedal into any prospects, he collapsed on the way.

On other people's four wheels is me, driving speedily;
Unable to drive out of danger, I am pressed for time.

(Trans: W. H. Hsu)

八行書

有風的景不應寂寥的。
時間如風帶走
歌，唱不散憂愁
沿露流不進洶湧
所有季節的沈默
已偷去喧嘩的年紀
就是不甘老看到
骷髏演戲。

An Eight-lined Letter

A scenery in the breeze should not be desolate.
Time like the wind is whisking away
The song that cannot dissipate woes;
Even with dew it cannot flow into surges.
The reticence of all seasons.
Has stolen years of uproar.
I simply refuse to take a glance
Of human skeletons' historionics.

(Trans: W. H. Hsu)

反調

怕單調的鳥飛遠了
肯做島的就不怕衝擊

一般仍模仿草默讀
不再活潑的土
節奏是顫慄

溪哽咽流不動天空
海咆哮太陽煮不滾

冷，靜起的
火是熱情的聲音
燃燒，嚷成灰燼

Discordant Tunes

Birds averse to monotony have flown away.
The island is inclined to repulse and assault.

People in general still imitate the grass reading
The land that livens up no longer.
Rhythm is shudder.

The brook chokes with incapability to move the sky.
The sea clamors against the sun for failing to boil.

Coldness will give rise to
The flame, a burning sound
Bursts into ashes.

(Trans: W. H. Hsu)

濁水溪畔

起初也清潔大雪山拋棄島腰的鞭越揮越渾了
農夫兒女的農夫兒女農夫搶救木材不再回來
農夫兒女的農夫兒女工人搶救機器不再回來
農夫兒女的農夫兒女學者擁抱知識不再回來
農夫兒女的農夫兒女商人擁抱錢財不再回來
還回不去，農夫兒女的農夫兒女老兵鄉愁肥沃

灌溉不出根
還未出去，農夫兒女的農夫兒女
踩自己的影子遊戲，輪騎自己

Beside the Muddy Water River

A whip brandished by the originally clean Great Snow mountain
is getting muddier.
Peasants, the children of the peasants' children,
who rescued timber, could no longer come back.
Workers, the children of the peasants' children,
who rescued machines, could no longer come back.
Scholars, the children of the peasants' children,
who embrace knowledge, would no longer come back.
Merchants, the children of the peasants' children,
who embrace money, would no longer come back.
Still unable to go back, the homesickness of the
soldiers, who are the children of the peasants' children, is fertile

But irrigates no root.
Still at home the children of the peasants' children play,
Treading their own shadows
   and taking turns to ride upon themselves.

(Trans: W. H. Hsu)

見聞

蟑螂吃饑民圖
吃掉嘴了仍無血肉
一孔又一孔又一孔
填上腥臭

Hear and See

Cockroaches eat a picture of famine victims,
Whose mouths have been eaten.
Yet no blood and flesh appear.
Hole and hole and hole
Are stuffed with stench.

(Trans: W. H. Hsu)

曾貴海
Tseng Kuei Hai
1946 ～

台灣屏東人，現居高雄。高雄醫學院醫科畢業，胸腔內科
醫師。現為「笠」詩社社長，並積極投入綠色環保運動、
參與台灣南方社運。
詩集《鯨魚的祭典》、《高雄詩抄》、《台灣男人的心事》、
《原鄉・夜合》等，並有散文，評論文集多冊。以詩及行動
介入社會改革，在抒情與批評之間呈顯文學心靈的多重交
會。

Tseng Kuei Hai (1946-) was born in Pingtung. Graduated
from Kaohsiung Medical College, he has practiced internal
medicine in Kaohsiung since 1973. Current editor-in-chief
of the *Li Poetry*, he has constantly engaged himself in local
environmental issues and social movements. His books of
poems include *The Sacrificial Ritual of Whales* (1983), *Poems
from Kaohsiung* (1986), *In the Mind of a Taiwanese Man* (1999)
and *Night Meeting in Native Village* (2000). Other publications
of essays and commentaries, as well as his poetry, highlight the
multiple concerns of a poet and activist.

鎖匙

不知道哪個病人
匆匆忙把藥拿走
卻留給我一串鎖匙

翻看著它
像是外科醫生手中的斷肢吧

失去了枷鎖
能夠在這水泥木板和鋼鐵的城市
活下去嗎

休診後把它掛在鐵柵門外
或許他正奔馳在秋末冷清無聲的街道
追尋

門等著他

Keys

I don't know which one of my patients
left me a set of keys in his hurry
after picking up a prescription

I examined them
as if they were some mutilated limbs

Can he survive
in this city of cement, lumber and steel
without the keys to his pillories and locks

I hung them outside the iron gate after closing
he might be searching for them up and down
on the desolate street of last autumn

a door is waiting for him

(Trans: William Marr)

公園

不想遺棄城市的母親
孤獨地守在一隅
讓迷失的孩子
需要愛時，靜靜地
走進她的懷抱

偶而思念起母親的孩子
路過家門
猶豫了一下
又發動車子追向街尾

找遍這個喧鬧的城市
污塵和廢氣飛揚的路旁
我看到一些
憂傷而木然的棄婦

A Park

A mother reluctant to desert the city
guards one corner by herself,
so that her stray child
in need of love
can quietly come back to her bosom.

The child who occasionally thinks of his mother
passes by the gate of his own home,
hesitates for a while
and then restarts the car chasing toward the end of the street.

Having searched through this clamorous city,
I discover, by the roadside in clouds of dust and waste gas,
deserted women stupefied and sorrowful.

(Trans: K. C. Tu)

荒村夜吠

寒冬的夜晚
冷風禁錮著整個僻靜的荒村

看不見人影
抖縮在屋角的
狗
無可選擇地
向四週深遠的幽暗
反擊

此刻，迴響著我心中
生於人世的冷冷的吠聲

Barking at Night in a Deserted Village

In a cold winter night
the bleak wind imprisons the whole deserted village.

Not a soul can be seen.
A shivering dog
huddles up at the corner of a house,
and attacks instinctively
the remote and profound darkness in all directions.

At this moment there echoes in my heart
a cold barking that came into this world.

(Trans: K. C. Tu)

鯨魚的祭典

追隨某種不為人知的訊息
衝上昨夜平靜的海灘
一大群鯨魚
排列在浪濤喚不回的岸邊
像一具具活的棺屍
等待日落後長夜的吞噬

初陽浮雕出牠們巨大的形體
春風自遠處吹過
心驚的人類
目觸集體的自棄
遙望那遼闊幽深的海洋
那時而平靜時而呼嘯的海洋
靈魂不知歸向何處

像著名的祭典儀式
在時間的輪帶上重複上演
當某首歌完全佔據了心靈
就大聲梵唱走前去
不管那裡是山是海是火
或是血

Rites of Whales

As if responding to some message unknown to man
a group of whales
rushed up the beach last night
and lay there in a row
their enormous bodies startled us
under the morning sun

Where are their souls roaming now
in the boundless ocean?
are they stirred as easily as the ocean?

Rites of sacrifice
repeatedly appear on time's stage
when a certain song fills the hearts
they all have to sing aloud and march forward
be it mountain or ocean or fire or blood

(Trans: William Marr)

小雞

母雞帶小雞
母雞最疼愛的是那隻
高大雄壯
羽毛漂亮的小公雞
啼起來比誰都響亮

但是，最先離牠而去的也是那隻

Little Chicks

A mother hen is watching her little chicks
she loves the tall and strong one most
the one with beautiful feathers
the one that sings the loudest

But, sadly, he is also the one
who will be first to leave

(Trans: William Marr)

李敏勇
Lee Min Yung
1947～

台灣屏東人，在高高屏成長，現居台北。大學時代修習歷史，以文學為志業。曾任《笠》詩刊主編。在文學、文化與社會運動多方介入。

詩集《鎮魂歌》、《野生思考》、《戒嚴風景》、《傾斜的島》、《心的奏鳴曲》、《自白書》等，並有散文隨筆，文化與社會評論集多冊，譯讀世界詩隨筆集多冊。抒情與批評兼具，藝術與社會並重，被視為持有發亮瞳孔，善於表達觀念的詩人以及詩的信使。

Lee Min Yung (1947-) was born in Kaohsiung. A history major, he began to publish poetry in 1967. A poet, critic and social activist, he has served as editor-in-chief of the *Li Poetry* and was president of Taiwan PEN. Winner of 2007 National Arts Award in literature, he has published several books of poems, essays and translations. His poetry collections include *Requiem* (1990), *The Wildlife Thinking* (1990), *Landscapes under Martial Law* (1990), *A Tilted Island* (1993), *Sonata in Soul* (1999) and *A Poet's Confession* (2009). He has also compiled many volumes of poetry by Taiwanese poets. His works feature a strong sense of commitment to society and reflection on the ethics of aesthetics.

浮標

我的國籍已無
這不是我的罪
也不是我的願望

我的傷痕
像海溝那樣深
累積了
世界最暗鬱的悲哀

我希冀
體會岸邊
浸染愛

可是
國土出現了又消失

Floating Beacon

I have lost my nationality ——
It is not my fault
Nor my wish

My scar
Deep as the ocean floor
Has been gathering
The darkest sorrows of the world

My burning desire
Is to feel the shore
And to soak in love

But again and again
The shore has appeared and disappeared
The banishment has been lifted and re-imposed

(Trans: William Marr)

夢

夜黑以後
現實有一個缺口
我是打那兒
逃亡的

像監禁終身犯一樣地
雖然你
監禁著我的一生

然而
逃亡以後的我
是自由的

你不能捕獲我愛的掌紋
你不能捕獲我恨的足跡

Dream

After nightfall
There was a crack in reality
Through which
I escaped

Although you
Had imprisoned me
Like a convict sentenced to life

I was free
After the escape

You could not capture the lines of my palms of love
You could not capture the traces of my feet of hatred

(Trans: William Marr)

底片的世界

關上門窗
拉上簾幕
我們拒絕一切破壞性的光源
在暗房裡
小心翼翼地
打開相機匣子
取出底片
它拍攝我們生的風景
從顯像到隱像
它記錄我們死的現實
從經驗到想像
我們小心翼翼地
把底片放進顯影藥水
以便明晰一切
它描繪我們生的歡愉
以相反的形式
它反映我們死的憂傷
以黯澹的色調
直到一切彰顯
我們才把底片取出
放進定影藥水
它負荷我們生的愛
以特殊的符號
它承載我們死的恨
以複雜的構成

The World of Negatives

Shut the windows and doors
pull down the shades
cut off all destructive light
in the darkroom
we open the camera carefully
and take out the negatives
they capture the scenery of our lives
making the visible invisible
they record the reality of our deaths
turning experience into fantasy
we carefully put
the negatives into the developer
so they can paint
the joys of our lives
in positive shapes
or describe the sorrows of our deaths
with obscure colors
when all the details appear
we remove the negatives
and put them into the fixer
they carry the love of our lives
in special symbols
they bear the hatred of our deaths
in complex forms
from this moment on

這時候
我們釋放所有的警覺
把底片放入清水
以便洗滌一切污穢
過濾一切雜質
純純粹粹把握證據
在歷史的檔案
追憶我們的時代

we don't need to be so careful
we rinse the negatives with clean water
and when the impurities are washed away
and the stains gone
we will be able to recollect our time
with pure proofs from the file of history

(Trans: William Marr)

從有鐵柵的窗

記得嗎
那天
下著雨的那天
我們站在屋內窗邊
你朗讀了柳致環的一首詩
　「……
　　……
唉！沒人能告訴我嗎？
究竟是誰？是誰首先想到
把悲哀的心掛在那麼高的天空？」
順手指著一面飄搖在雨中被遺忘的旗
很傷感的樣子
而我
我要你看對街屋簷下避雨的一隻鴿子
牠正啄著自己的羽毛
偶而也走動著
牠抬頭看天空
像是在等待雨停後要在天空飛翔
我們撫摸著冰涼的鐵柵
它監禁著我們
說是為了安全
我們撫摸著它
想起家家戶戶都依賴它把世界關在外面
不禁悲哀起來
從有鐵柵的窗

From the Window behind the Iron Bars

Do you remember
that day
that rainy day
when we stood beside the window
you recited a poem by Yu Chih Huan
"......................

....
ai! can no one tell me who?
who was the first one to think of
hanging a dejected spirit high on the sky?"
and pointed to a forgotten flag flapping in the rain
looking very sad indeed
and I
I wanted you to see the pigeon hiding under the eaves
across the street
it was pecking at its own feathers
occasionally pacing a few steps
and looking at the sky
as if it was waiting for the rain to stop so it
could soar high again into the sky
we stroked the icy iron bars
they imprisoned us
for the sake of our security
we stroked them
and were saddened

我們封鎖著自己
我們拒絕真正打開窗子
讓陽光和風進來
我們不去考慮鐵柵的象徵
它那麼荒謬地嘲弄著我們
它使得我們甚至不如一隻鴿子
牠在雨停後
飛躍到天空自由的國度裡
而我們
我們僅能望著那面潮濕的旗
想像著或許我們的心是隨著那鴿子
盤旋在雨後潔淨透明的天空

註：柳致環，韓國詩人，「……」內的詩句是他詩作〈旗〉的結尾。

to think of all the families depending on them
  to shut the world out
we locked ourselves up
behind the iron bars
we refused to really open the windows
to let in sunshine and the winds
we didn't want to think of the symbols they represent
they jeered at us
they made us even worse off than a pigeon
after the rain stops
the pigeon can fly in the free sky
while we can only stare at the damp flag
and imagine ourselves flying with the pigeon
in the rain-washed, pellucid sky

(Trans: William Marr)

風景

從逐漸死去的河口
仍然聽得到海的聲音
核污染的廢水
在那兒和海相會

從撫慰我們的天空
仍然看得見雀鳥的飛行
核污染的浮塵
在那兒謀殺雀鳥

從枯黃的原野
仍然摘得到野菊的花客
核污染的陰影
在那兒籠罩野菊

從核電廠
描繪出硝煙的風景
描繪出繃帶的風景
描繪出腐敗的風景

Landscapes

At the mouth of a dying river
The sound of the ocean still can be heard.
There, nuclear waste water
meets the ocean.

In the sky that consoles us
birds can still be seen flying.
There, nuclear fallout
murders the birds.

In the wild field that is withered and yellow
blooming mother chrysanthemums can still be gathered.
There, the shadow of nuclear pollution
envelops the chrysanthemums.

The nuclear power plant is portraying
a landscape with gunpowder smoke
a landscape bandaged.
a landscape decayed.

(Trans: K. C. Tu)

邊界

島嶼沒有邊界
環繞蔚藍的海洋

島嶼沒有邊界
籠罩亮麗的天空

是誰弄成銅鐵的邊界啊

刺網
限制了航行的憧憬

柵欄
限制了飛翔的希望

Boundaries

An island surrounded by the blue ocean
has no boundary.

An island under the bright sky
has no boundary.

Also, who are they
building the bastion of iron to delimit boundaries?

The barbed wires
restrict the yearning for long voyages.

The boom nets
restrict the hope of flying free.

(Trans: K. C. Tu)

在世紀之橋的禱詞

戰火成為歷史
災難成為記憶
傷痕與淚珠形成自然的簾幕
在薄雨中呈顯
一座彩虹像世紀之橋
在時間的盡頭和起點
分隔過去和未來
現在是
世紀末的黃昏
入夜後
星星會指引我們
穿越黑暗
從水平線透露的光照耀日昇之屋
福爾摩沙依然在海的懷抱裡
釀造夢想
地平線上
她的子民共同呼喚
台灣的名字

A Prayer at the Bridge between the Centuries

War is consigned to histoy

Disaster to memory

The scars and tears form a natural screen

In a drizzle

A rainbow appears like a bridge between the centuries

At the end and the beginning of time

Separating past and future

Now it is

Dusk at century's end

After the fall of night

The stars will point the way

Through the darkness

The light on the horizon shines on the house of the rising sun

Formosa remains in the sea's embrace

Brewing dreams

Above the horizon

Together, her people call out

Taiwan

(Trans: John Balcom)

陳明台
Chen Ming Tai
1948～

台灣台中人，現居台中。大學時代修習歷史，日本筑波大學歷史人類學博士課程修畢。曾在淡江大學日文系，中正大學台灣文學研究所任教。父為「笠」詩社創辦人——詩人陳千武。

詩集《孤獨的位置》、《遙遠的鄉愁》、《風景畫》、評論集《心境與風景》等，譯介日本詩與戲劇、小說多冊。敏感而纖細的抒情風格，漂流情境以及歷史體認交集成作品特色。

Cheng Ming Tai (1948-) was born in Taichung. Son of poet Chen Chien Wu, he is also a critic and translator. A history major, he pursued further studies in the field of historical anthropology in Japan. He has taught in several universities in Taiwan. His publications include poetry collections *Position in Solitude* (1972), *Remote Nostalgia* (1985) and *A Landscape Painting* (1986), as well as translations of Japanese poetry, dramas and novels. His poetry is characteristic of a lyrical style with detached looks on man in time.

月

哀傷的月
睜大眼睛在注視
狹窄的血槽上依然滴著鮮血的劍
躺在乾硬的砂土上
陰森而寒冷　閃閃亮著青色的光的劍

哀傷的月
睜大眼睛在注視
瀕死的年輕的兵士
夢想遙遠的故鄉而闔不上眼睛的兵士
靈魂附著遠遠的星星顯得淒艷的兵士

哀傷的月
睜大眼睛在注視
暗將下來的戰場
剛剛經歷過激烈的搏鬥
疲憊下來的戰場
舐食散亂的肢體到處徘徊著狗的戰場

哀傷的月
睜大眼睛在注視
唯一的生還者的巨大的旗幟
飄在風中茫然的打顫的旗幟
緊緊地握在死去的少年的手中的旗幟

The Moon

The grieved moon
Gazes with big eyes.
The sword still drips with blood on the narrow trough.
Lying on the dried sand,
The sword, gruesome and cold, glitters with green light.

The grieved moon
Gazes with big eyes.
The soldier young but dying.
The soldier dreaming of home and unable to close his eyes.
The soldier whose soul adheres to the distant stars looks dreary.

The grieved moon
Gazes with big eyes.
The darkening battlefield
Has just gone through a fierce fight
The battlefled becomes weary.
The battlefield with dogs wandering about licking scattered bodies.

The grieved moon
Gazes with big eyes.
The only survivor's huge flag.
The flag fluttering in the air and shuddering blankly.
The flag held on tightly in the hand of a dead boy.

而不知道從什麼地方
昇起來的含淚的母親的臉
仰起頭在注視
高高地掛在敗北的灰色的天空上
漸漸被朦朧的烟霧模糊了的
哀傷的月

深遠的夜　染得更黑了
沉浸在破滅的生的風景裡

From somewhere
Rises the mother's tearful face.
She looks up
At the grieved moon
Loftily hanging in the gray, defeated sky
And becoming blurred with mist.

The far and deep night is dyed even darker.
And soaked in the scene of shattered life.

(Trans: K. C. Tu)

天空和枯枝和女人的聲音

秋天曾經是晴朗的涼爽的天空
冬天曾經是美麗的裝飾的枯枝
女人的聲音曾經是溫暖的充滿的喜悅

像受傷的小鳥
女人從高高深遠的天空
墜落而下
像切斷的枯枝
女人在蕭蕭的風裡
搖晃殘軀

打從那個事件的黃昏
女人的聲音是狂人的咀咒
女人的聲音是鬼女的呼號
秋天的暗鬱的天空是生的哀愁的象徵
冬天的乾癟的枯枝是死的僵凍的形狀

The Sky, Dead Trees, and the Woman's Voice

Autumn once was a sunny, nice and cool sky.

Winter once was decorated with beautiful, dead trees.

The woman's voice once was full of warmth of joy.

Like a wounded bird,

The woman from the high and remote sky,

Fell down.

Like a broken, dead tree,

The woman in the soughing wind

Sways the remains of her body.

Since the evening of the incident,

The woman's voice has become a maniac's curse

The woman's voice has become a ghost's crying.

The sky of the gloomy autumn, a symbol of the sorrow of life.

The withered trees in the dried winter, the body of frozen death.

(Trans: K. C. Tu)

風景畫

潑墨的雲底下是
蒼鬱的山巒
覆上了一層白
山巒的底下是
無限伸展的曠野
覆上了一層白

雪　還是在積降著
那一天
一起跋涉在無人的小徑
異國籍的兄弟
兩個人的足跡
那麼清晰地印在心底
印在似乎是延綿無盡的路上

多麼渴望火啊
交互的飲了水壺中剩下的少許的燒酒
平安回到家時
請相互珍重友誼
發出訊息　不要中斷

誠摯地　交換了約定
那是五年前的舊事

A Landscape Painting

Beneath ink-splashed clouds are
Verdant mountains
Covered with white
Beneath the mountains is
A boundless wilderness
Covered with white

Snow was still falling
On that day
Brothers of different countries
Strolled on the deserted path
Their footsteps
Clearly printed in their hearts
On the seemingly endless road

They desired fire
And mutually drank little warm wine from a bottle
When they came home safely
They treasured their friendship
Promising to keep in touch

Cordially they exchanged the agreement
That was the old affair five years ago

現在是
全然　音訊不明
也許　有一天　驚異的訃聞會……

兩隻眼睛　凝視在
畫上了　昨天踩下的腳印
貼在牆上
一張　樸素的
風景畫

不忍心轉移目標
畫裡
雪　冷冷地　還是在積降著

Now completely no news at all
Perhaps someday a surprised funeral will.....

Two eyes stare at
The painting, yesterday's footsteps
Are sticked on the wall
A simple
Landscape painting

I cannot bear to divert my attention
On the painting
Snow is still falling with coldness

(Trans: W. H. Hsu)

海

不斷地吹拂的海風打亂了髮絲
冷清清的海濱的小鎮的早期
只有掛在竹竿上的魚網
無聊地晃蕩著

突然　遠方的駛進來
龐大的觀光巴士
跟隨舉著旗子的嚮導
大群的行列步出車站
一瞬間　不知在哪兒
消失了蹤影

屹立在街道的兩旁
矮小的木屋的前面
婦人們顯現了瘦削的身子
默默地開始一天的工作
無視周遭的一切
機械地晒著魚在木架上
在防波堤上坐著
聽得見波濤捲起浪花
遙遠的地平線
飄蕩過來母親層層疊疊的溫柔叮嚀

飄蕩過來母親層層疊疊的溫柔叮嚀
環繞著小鎮的四周
海的
無限的寂寥
在擴散著

Sea

Sea breezes kept disheveling hair,
In the old days of the desolate seaside town,
Only the fishnets hung on the bamboo poles
Swayed languidly.

All crowd stepped out of the stop,
Followed a guide holding a banner,
And disappeared in a distance.

In front of the small, low cottages
On the roadside
Emerged women's emaciated bodies
They quietly began their daily chores,
Mechanically drying fish on the wooden racks
Without noticing surroundings.
Sitting on the breakwater,
One heard spindrifts the waves produced,
And mothers' repeated affectionate callings the waves drifted
From the distant horizon.

Mothers' repeated affectionate callings the waves drifted
Encircled the town.
The boundless desolation of the sea was extending.

(Trans: K. C. Tu)

鄭烱明
Cheng Chiung Ming
1948 ～

台灣台南人，現居高雄。中山醫學大學醫科畢業，內科小兒科醫師。《文學台灣》發行人，並為文學台灣基金會董事長。
詩集《歸途》、《悲劇的想像》、《蕃薯之歌》、《最後的戀歌》、《三重奏》等。並主編《台灣精神的崛起——笠詩論選集》。在南台灣推動台灣文學發展，貢獻良多。

Cheng Chiung Ming (1948-) was born in Tainan. A medical physician based in Kaohsiung, he has initiated the publication of *Literary Taiwan* magazine in 1991, and became chairman of the Literary Taiwan Foundation. His collections of poetry include *A Homebound Journey* (1971), *The Imagination of Tragedy* (1976), *Song of Sweet Potato* (1981), *The Last Love Song* (1986) and *Trio* (2008). He was responsible for the compilation and publication of *The Rise of Taiwan Spirit*, a collections of essays, conference minutes and historic documents pertaining to *Li Poetry* magazine and society.

蕃薯

狠狠地
把我從溫暖的土裡
連根挖起
說是給我自由

然後拿去烤
拿去油炸
拿去烈日下曬
拿去煮成一碗一碗
香噴噴的稀飯

吃掉了我最營養的部分
還把我貧血的葉子倒給豬吃

對於這些
從前我都忍耐著
只暗暗怨嘆自己的命運
唉，誰讓我是一條蕃薯
人見人愛的蕃薯

但現在不行了
從今天開始
我不再沉默
我要站起來說話
以蕃薯的立場說話

Sweet Potato

They brutally dig me up
from the warmth of the soil
in order to
liberate me

then they bake me
fry me
boil me
dry me under the sun

they eat my most nutritious part
and give my anaemic leaves toe the pigs

I used to put up with all these things
It's my fate, I said to myself
the fate of being a delicious sweet potato

but now it's different
from now on
I will not keep my silence
I will stand up and say
from the standpoint of a sweet potato
whether you like it or not

I want to say it aloud

不管你願不願聽

我要說
對著廣闊的田野大聲說
請不要那樣對待我啊
我是無辜的
我沒有罪！

to the vast field
don't treat me like that
I am innocent
I am guiltless

(Trans: William Marr)

失踪

有一天，當我失踪
那可不是一件鬧著玩的事兒

有人會從圍牆內
迅速放出成群的猛犬
一路吠又嗅
夾著急促的步伐
向手電筒照射的叢林
找尋我的足跡

是誰在門口咆哮…
警戒森嚴
怎麼可能失踪？
莫非……

其實我只是悶得發慌
想向他們開玩笑
吃了一顆隱身丸
暫時躲了起來
我的靈魂仍乖乖廝守著
那屬於我的單調的房間
我沒有失踪

坐在地上
我暗自竊笑

Disappearance

The night when I disappeared
it was not a joking matter

Someone inside the walls immediately set free
a pack of hounds, howing and sniffing
together with the sound of hurrying footsteps
all directed by the flashlights
toward to jungle
to look for my footprints

Outside the door somebody roared:
how could he escape
under such tight security?
unless.....

In fact, I was merely playing a joke on them
out of bordom
a pill randered me invisible
while my soul was still confined
in my solitary room
I did not escape

I sat on the floor and laughed to myself
when they found me
upon their return from the exhausting expedition

什麼時候他們
一個一個疲憊地回來
發現我
然後把我痛打一頓
用他們的愚蠢

they would beat me up
with their stupidity

(Trans: William Marr)

旅程

從夢中出發
去尋找
不受污染的愛
是一次痛苦的旅程

當然
沒有經歷挫敗和恐怖的你
永遠無法理解
也無法想像

從夢中出發
穿過恨的鐵絲網
抵達目的地時
也許正在狂暴的沙漠中
也許正在燃燒的森林裡
無處可逃

這時，所有的希望
會化做一隻不死的鳥
沖出
飛向故鄉的天空
不再回來

A Journey

My departure from a dream
To search for
Unpolluted love
Is an agonizing journey.

Without any experience of defeat and horror,
You surely have no way to understand
Or to imagine.

After departing from my dream,
I pass through the barbwire of hatred.
When I reach my destination,
Perhaps it is a stormy desert,
Perhaps it is a burning forest.
I can escape nowhere.

At that juncture, all hopes
Will metamorphose into an immortal bird
And break out
To fly toward the sky of the home country
And never return again.

(Trans: W. S. Hsu)

三重奏

1 . 我

我不是你的一部分
因為我不是單純的我

我曾經擁有你
在不堪回首的歲月裡

請不要對我恫嚇
我的體內蘊藏你不瞭解的人生
明天，我將以另一個我

從透明的海岸出發

2 . 你

你不時窺視著我
以一雙狼的青色的眼睛

在寂靜無聲的夜裡
你暗藏的慾望膨脹
如巨蟒般
從海的那邊纏繞過來

你利用語言

Trio

1 . I

Not part of you, I am
All because I am not that simple

Once I owned you
In my anguished reminiscences

Stop intimidating me
With your perplexed life I cannot take
I will set out tomorrow

Anew from the translucent seashore

2 . **You**

Time and again you cast furtive glances at me
With the wolf's bluish eyes

At still night
Your subconscious desire extends
Like a boa
Snaking its way from the sea

You use language tediously

不厭其煩的
構築一個又一個
虛幻的世界

有人慶幸已經找到　出口

3．他

隔著海峽
他以毀滅性的武器瞄準我
然後微笑著說：我要擁抱你

我感覺到他亢奮的心跳
熟悉而陌生地
敲打我脆弱的耳膜

我的存在
是一種令人無法忍受之惡嗎？

灰色的海的天空
看不見一雙海鷗飛翔

To construct hallucinatory worlds one after another

Someone is congratulating himself
On his way out

3 . He

Across the straits
He aims at me with destructive weapons
And says all smiles: I will embrace you

I feel his agitated palpitations
Beating my soft ear drums
With familiar weirdness

Is my existence
His unbearable evil?

In the sky of the grayish sea
There is no any gull hovering in sight

(Trans: K. C. Tu)

莫渝
Mo Yu
1948～

台灣苗栗人，現居台北。淡江大學法文系畢業，曾任教
職，出版社主編，現為《笠》詩刊主編，在法國詩的漢譯
及兒童文學極有建樹。
詩集《土地的戀歌》、《浮雲集》、《水鏡》、《第一道曙
光》、《革命軍》等，譯編作品數量頗豐，對戰後台灣詩的
發展視野廣泛。

Mo Yu (1948-) is pen name of Lin Liang Ya. Born in Miaoli,
he majored in French in Taiwan, and studied translation in
France between 1982 and 1983. Having worked as a teacher
and book editor, he is currently editor-in-chief of the *Li Poetry*.
He is a translator into Chinese of French literature works and
major contributor to children's literature. His collections of
poems include *Love Song of the Earth* (1986), *Clouds* (1990),
The Mirror of the Water (1998), *The First Light of Day* (2007)
and *The Revolutionary Army* (2010). He has also compiled
numerous books that introduce Taiwanese poets and their
works.

父親靈前的焚稿

秋雨

秋天的雨，下得好淒涼
父親，讓我撐開雨傘
護送您走完最後的旅途
好久，我們不曾如此貼近

您儘管放心闔上眼瞼
這條路，我還熟悉
還能順利地護送您

父親
好久，我們不曾如此貼近
今夜，讓我們再次共撐這把
好久未撐開過的雨傘
當年
幼稚的我曾在傘下與您同行

燒香

已經是多年習慣了
每日晨昏固定時刻
總要向祖先的神位，與
屋外的青天
燒三柱香

Poems Burned in the Presence of My Father's Spirit

Autumn Rains

Autumn rains are desolate and sorrowful
on this last journey of yours, father
let me hold the umbrella for you
we have not been so close for a long time

you can just close your eyes and relax
I am still familiar with this path
and can accompany you safely to your destination

we have not been so close for a long time,
father
tonight let us share the umbrella
that has not been used since the year
when I, as a youth,
shared it with you

Incense Burning

It was a habit of many years
every morning at fixed hour
you would burn three sticks of incense
before the ancestral tablet
and the heavens

不曾聽到口中念念的詞句
但虔誠的姿勢一絲不苟
正像您待人處事的平凡一生

您走了，父親，請放心
神明與青天的香燭
還會繼續延燒下去
繼續傳述兒子的心語

I did not hear any prayers
yet your gesture of sincerity
always reminded me of your simple and serious life

now you are gone, father, but please don't worry
the incense will continue to be burned
to honor the ancestors and the heavens
and to cover you son's innermost feelings

(Trans: William Marr)

凝窗的露水

清晨，拉開布幔
準備歡迎欣然的陽光

外宿整夜的露水
卻早先一步映入眼簾
緊貼窗玻璃
彷彿被慢待的你
把濃重濃重的相思
化作楚楚可憐的露水
凝窗且沿窗緩緩流下
盯住暗自埋怨的我

Dewdrops on Window Panes

I drew up the curtains in the morning
to welcome the joyous sun

the dewdrops, staying out all night,
were the first ones to come in
they clung to the windowpanes
as if you, the neglected one,
had turned your ponderous lovesickness
into the pitiful dewdrops
condensed on the windowpanes and slowly
dripping down
you stared at me soaked in my self-reproach

(Trans: William Marr)

花市

路過花市
吾愛
我買下一盆小花
讓自己快樂
讓遠方的你知道我快樂

路過花市
吾愛
想你該在我右邊
欣賞這些鮮艷的秋景
我們家鄉一樣有

路過異國花市
吾愛，我忍不住地
逗留又逗留
想在群花當中
找尋一張熟悉的面孔

Flower Market

Passing by the flower market
my love
I bought a small pot of flowers
to make myself happy
to let you know that I am happy

Passing by the flower market
my love
thinking that you should have been at my side
to enjoy this colorful autumnal scene
as we used to enjoy in our hometown

Passing by the flower market in a foreign land
my love, I can't help
lingering and lingering
hoping to find a familiar face
among the flowers

(Trans: William Marr)

黃昏鳥

抬眼，又是另一種天色逼視
仿佛寡歡的散雲緊鎖
一山的眉聚
來不及讓左岸的夕陽蒸暖

硬被這種莫可奈何扣結
今夕，我們落宿悽涼
在承受不起過重思維的枝椏上
或者，繼續前程
投向燈盞亮處

不為迷失，而是沒有歸途
我們瞇起眼睛
茫視蜃樓般誘引的前端

前端，沒有燈火的
冷冷

Birds at Dusk

Looking up, another color of sky peers down
As if the unhappy scattered clouds knit
The mountain's brows
Too late for warmth from the sun setting over the left bank

We have no alternative but being detained
Tonight, do we lodge drearily
On flimsy branches that cannot bear a weighty thought
Or keep on our journey
In search of a bright, well-lit place

Not because we are lost, but because we have no way home
We fix our eyes ahead
On that mirage leading us on

Up ahead, the cold
Darkness

(Trans: John Balcom & Yingtsih Huang)

江自得
Chiang Tzu The
1948～

台灣台中人，現居台中。高雄醫學院醫科畢業，胸腔內科
醫師，曾任《笠》詩刊社長，並參與台灣中部的文化與社
會運動。
詩集《那天，我輕輕觸著了妳的傷口》、《故鄉的太陽》、
《從聽診器的那端》、《遙遠的悲哀》、《Ilha Formosa》等。
並有散文集《漂泊──在醫學與人文之間》。顯現醫療的視
野，觀照社會。觸探台灣歷史，開拓史詩的情境。

Chiang Tze The (1948-) was born in Taichung. A chest
physician by profession, he retired from his post as head of the
Section of Internal Medicine of Taichung Veterans Hospital in
2003. He was president of *Li Poetry* society and cofounded the
Literary Taiwan quarterly in 1991. He is now chairman of the
Taiwan Medicine and Humanity Foundation. His publications
include *That Day I Touched Tenderly Your Wound* (1990), *Sun
of My Hometown* (1992), *From the End of the Stethoscope*
(1996), *Distant Sorrow* (2006) and *Ilha Formosa* (2010). His
poetry feels the pulse of human being, the Taiwanese society
and its history.

咳嗽

曾經，你說過
故鄉漆黑的深處
蘊藏著
大地咳嗽的聲音

曾經，你說過
人類基因庫的底層
蘊藏著
悲哀的眼淚
喔！日夜漂流的你
在死滅的土地
在污濁的街道

在核爆的陰影
在權勢的網結
在物慾的洪流中
日夜漂流的你，終於
對著不可測的命運
拋出一串串
憤怒的咳嗽

第一聲是
　　牙刷主義
第二聲是
　　黨國資本主義

Cough

Once upon a time, you spoke
Of the pitch-black depths of the countryside,
Pent up:
The sound of the great earth's cough.

Once upon a time you spoke
Of the deep layer of the human gene pool
Pent up:
The teardrops of woe.
Oh! Day and night with you afloat
About the extinguished earth
About the dirty streets

About the shadow of the nuclear blast,
About the network of power and influence,
About the flood of material desire.
Day and night do you float, finally
In the face of your unfathomable fate,
Cast out one and all,
Cough of wrath.

The first sound is
Toothbrushism.*
The second sound is
Party-nation capitalism.

第三聲是
　　他媽的爛主義
　　…………

The third sound is
Lousy worthlessnessism.

....

*A term often appearing in the headlines in the 1970s, "toothbrushism" referred to the practice of preparing for an invasion from China.

(Trans: W. H Hsu)

心臟移植

為了接納你的心
我脫去一層又一層
深厚如繭的自負

你用最沉潛的體溫
輕輕撫過
我體內每一個細胞

從這一刻起
我把你的心珍藏
在往後的人生裡

而我清楚地聽見
一種聲音
在內心不停地叫喊

噢！那必是我們倆的命運
在世界最深邃的某處
相互撞擊的聲響

Heart Transplant

To receive your heart
I divest the thick cocoon of my conceit
Layer upon layer.

With latent body temperature
You gently feel
Every cell of my flesh.

Since then
I have treasured your heart
In the remainder of my life.

I clearly hear
A voice
Crying out in my heart incessantly

Oh, that must be the sound of the touch
Of our common lot
In some place in the deep of the world

(Trans: W. H. Hsu)

遺傳基因

美麗的花朵
　準時
在春天怒放
枯黃的樹葉
　準時
在秋天凋零

如此遞嬗了多少寒暑
在人間

總有人辯証
善與惡
總有人爭奪
歷史與意義

總有瘟疫流行
在世紀末的大地

Genes

Lovely flowers
Bloom in profusion in spring
On schedule.
Withered tree leaves
Flutter in autumn
On schedule.

Such alternation of the seasons transpires
In the human world.

Some people would apply dialectics
In good and evil.
Some people would scramble
For history and significance.

The plague always prevails
In the great earth toward the end of the century

(Trans: K. C. Tu)

從聽診器的那端

冬天的早晨空蕩蕩
冷風吹得很懶散
一陣孤寂自亙古的洪荒向你襲來
籠罩著沉甸甸的烏雲的天空
開始感到些許焦躁不安的天空
因而抱怨起俄羅斯的政變，喬治亞的內戰
德國統一後的紛亂及蕭條景象

病中的早晨陰暗暗
思緒湧現得很靦腆
陣陣雨絲落在你傾斜的回憶裡
蟠踞著黑魆魆的愛滋病毒的軀體
開始爆漲崩裂的軀體
因而憎恨起人類的偏狹，無盡的慾望
好勇鬥狠的習性

從聽診器的那端
我在你生命的底層細細傾聽
依稀聽到你DNA傳來的死亡密碼
緊扣住遠方世界爭執的聲音

From the Other End of the Stethoscope

A winter morning empty and calm
a cold wind blowing languidly
a burst of loneliness assails you from primitive antiquity
A sky enveloped in leaden clouds
a sky that starts to feel somewhat restless with anxiety
thus starts to complain about the coup d'etat in Russia,
the civil war in Georgia.
the chaos and depression after German unification

A morning during illness dismal and dark
various thoughts emerging timidly
bursts of fine rain fall into your slanting remembrance
A body crawling with the black nightmarish virus of AIDS
a body that starts to burst and break apart
thus comes to have human beings' illiberality, endless desire
and bellicose nature

From the other end of the stethoscope
I am carefully listening at the bottom of your life
to the secret code of death vaguely transmitted from your DNA
closely tied together with the fighting noise of the world from afar

(Trans: Robert Backus & K. C. Tu)

孟買海灘的老人

皺紋如背後的海浪
一波波湧上前額
胸前垂掛著幾包乾果和香煙糖
背後馱著的是
古銅色的黃昏，以及
阿拉伯海

我問他香煙糖一包多少錢
他卻用一種石灰質的笑容
向我兜售
海，以及
斑駁的歲月

An Old Man on a Bombay Beach

Wrinkles like waves behind

Keep dashing on his forehead.

Several packs of dried fruits and nicotine candies dangle on his chest

He carries on his back

Brazen dusk

As well as the Arabian Sea.

I enquire about the price of the nicotine candies.

With a face wreathed in slaked-lime smiles

He hawks

The sea and motley time.

(Trans: K. C. Tu)

陳鴻森
Chen Hung Sen
1950～

台灣高雄人，現居台北。中研院史語所研究員，從事中國漢代經學史及清代學術史研究，並在大學文學所任教。
詩集《期嚮》、《雕刻字的兒子》、《陳鴻森詩存》等。曾主編《笠120期作品刊目》，並推動《時代的眼，現實之花——笠1～120期普印本》出刊。詩作富生命實感和反逆思考，借喻比喻，探討文化、歷史、政治。

Chen Hung Sen (1950-) was born in Kaohsiung. A research fellow at the Institute of History and Philology of Taiwan's Academia Sinica, he is specialized in the history of the study of Chinese classics and academic history of the Qing Dynasty, and has taught in various Taiwanese institutes. He is author of poetry collections *Expectations* (1970), *Sculptor's Son* (1976) and *Poems by Chen Hung Sen* (2005). He was the driving force behind the reproduction of the *Li Poetry*'s historic issues No. 1 to 120. His poetry deals with culture, history and politics using varied metaphors and metonyms.

比目魚

由於不同的視界和意識型態
比目魚終於宣告分裂
成為左右各別的兩個個體
牠們各自拖著半邊的虛幻
踉蹌地　向著自己視界裡的海域

左邊的鮃　永遠看不到
牠的右方還有海原的存在
右邊的鰈　也同樣否定了
牠左方的現實
牠們互本指控著　對方的背反
三十多年來
一直共有著同一名字的　左鮃右鰈
由於異向的游程
牠們之間終於形成了
一個寂寥的海峽

日日迎衝著橫逆的潮
鮃的右眼因而逐漸右移
回到了牠身軀的右側
鰈的左眼亦逐漸地左移
而回到牠身軀的左側

如今，這已不再比目而行的鮃與鰈
除了牠們先後移動過的眼

Flounders

Due to different visions and ideologies, a
flounder has finally declared division of itself
into two separate bodies, one left-eyed and
the other right-eyed, each dragging half of the
illusion and staggeringly swimming toward
the ocean within its own vision.

The left-eyed flounder can never see that on
its light side there is ocean; the right-eyed
flounder likewise denies the reality on its left side.
Both accuse each other of treachery.
For more than thirty years
they have shared the same name,
but because of the opposite courses
they take, finally a lonely strait is formed
between them.

Day after day met and assailed by turbulent
waves, the left-eyed flounder's right eye gradually
moves to the right and returns to the right side
of its body; the right-eyed flounder's left eye also
gradually moves to the left, and returns to the left side of its body.

And now the left-eyed and right-eyed flounders
are not paralleling themselves eye to eye any more.

略覺木然外
牠們的形態
則日益相——似

Except for their newly dislocated eyes that
somehow feel dull, their forms have become
more and more similar to each other.

(Trans: K. C. Tu)

漁父吟

今天不出海
讓我們看
解放軍用導彈炸魚去

這裡是我們的土地
那邊是我們的海域
是我們賴以維生的漁場

捕魚半生
如今　才驚覺
自己也是魚肉

流連中國海的魚群
倉皇奔竄，在那被劫掠的海峽
思索著「祖國」的意義

官未能護漁
官不能守土
然而　官不怕食無魚

A Fisherman's Chant

We do not set sail today.
Let's go and see
The People's Liberation Army blowing up fish with guided missiles.

Our land is here.
Over there are our sea areas,
The fishing grounds on which we make a living.

I have been fishing for half of my lifetime now
Only to find with a start
That I myself am also the flesh of the fish.

Schools of fish lingering in to East China Sea
Disperse in a flurry in the looted strait,
Pondering the meaning of "Fatherland."

Officials are unable to protect fishing.
Officials are unable to defend the land.
They nevertheless do not worry about having no fish to eat.

(Trans: K. C. Tu)

校勘學
——讀莊子

魯魚亥豕
每下愈況
我們尋行數墨
反覆推敲
不敢稍有輕忽，甚至是
十目一行

此亦一是非
彼亦一是非
沿途盡是歧義的人生
審時度勢
權衡再三
像外文辭令般
字斟句酌的
就是不敢輕下案斷

在我們的時代
左右形似
虛實相似
積非成是　聚是成非
要勘正訛誤
談
何容易

Textual Criticism

Copying errors
Get worse each time
We stick to the words and not the meaning
Deliberating again and again
Never daring to neglect, ten eyes
Go over each and every line

This is also disputed
That is also disputed
In life there are different shades of meaning
Again and again we
Study and weigh the situation
Again and again we consider
Deliberating over words and expressions
as if they were diplomatic language
Never drawing hasty conclusions

In our time
Left and right are similar
Right and wrong are similar
Many mistakes make it right many rights make it wrong
To proofread and correct
Easier said
Than done

心非口是　唯唯
昨是今非　諾諾
是是非非
形形色色
孰非？
孰是？
欲辨已忘

Saying 'yes' means 'no' "Yes! Yes!"
What was right in the past is wrong today "Okay! Okay!"
The right and the wrong
Come in every shape and color
Which is wrong?
Which is right?
We've forgotten how to discriminate.

(Trans: John Balcom & Yingtsih Huang)

郭成義
Kuo Cheng Yi
1950～

台灣基隆人，現居台北。曾任《笠》詩刊主編，從事出版
與雜誌編輯，在《自由時報》擔任撰述委員。
詩集《薔薇的血跡》、《台灣民謠的苦悶》、《國土》等，
評論集《從抒情趣味到反藝術思想》。策劃主編《笠》叢書
《台灣詩人選集三十冊》。作品富機智，具深刻人性反思與
批評精神。

Kuo Cheng Yi (1950-) was born in Keelung. Having worked
for publishing companies and magazines, he was once editor-
in-chief of *Li Poetry*. Based in Taipei, he is now an editorial
writer for Chinese-language newspaper *Liberty Times*. His
publications include *The Bloodstain of a Rose* (1975), *The
Agony of Taiwanese Folk Song* (1986) and *The National Land*
(2010). He led the compilation of 30 volumes of poetry by
major Taiwanese poets published by the *Li Poetry* society. His
poetry provides witty and critical reflections on human nature.

雨夜花

只因為溫柔
才移根到這小小的地方
慢慢被修剪成
水仙一樣孤獨的花

在仰望雨露的花瓣上
我夜夜不休的織著
幾絲纖長而浪漫的夢
竟越來越深了

沒有人知道
夢是只有在雨夜裡才看得見的花
我終於在落雨的昨夜
赤裸地綻開了
脈脈含淚的花瓣

只是
有人說
昨夜確曾聽到
我斷氣的聲音

A Flower on a Rainy Night

For being gentle and meek,
I was transplanted to this small place
and gradually prunded into
a lonely flower like a narcissus.

On the petals that long for rain and dew,
I keep weaving night after night
some tenuous and amorous dreams
which turn out to be longer and deeper.

Nobody knows
dreams are the flowers visible only on a rainy night.
Last night it was raining,
I finally bloomed nakedly
with unbidden tears falling on the petals.

Yet somebody admitted that
last night he heard
the sound of my last breath.

(Trans: K. C. Tu)

領結的美學

被拘禁在商店
的玻璃室裡
而把假人的脖子
殺死了的
黑領結
有時是浮現在
被映照的我的頸間

灌滿著
暴力美學的領結
有時溫柔的手上
竟被染出

懸虛的那空缺
成為一個暗殺的現場
只出神地瞭望著
對世界充滿溫柔的
美的幻想的
那個人

Aesthetics of a Bowtie

Detained inside the glass
Of a shopwindow,
A black bowtie
Has strangled the mannequin to death
But sometimes appears
On my reflected neck.

Filled with aesthetics of violence,
A bowtie sometimes
Absconds from the gentle hands.

The empty position it left
Has become the scene of a murder.
Held spellbound and gazing afar,
That man, full of gentle
And beautiful fantasy
Toward the world.

(Trans: K. C. Tu)

行李

被遺忘在
慢行的長途列車上
一口載重的
行李

我獨自思索著
裡面所存放的物品
而感到那些
一再被盥洗的羞恥
不斷地疊增著
竟至喪失了
尋回它的勇氣

靜靜的
什麼地方
一口打著名字的行李
猶自幽冥地
旅行著呢

A Piece of Luggage

Has been forgotten on
A slow-moving, long distance train
A heavy peice of
Luggage

Alone, I think about
Its contents
And feel the
Shame washed out again and again
Keeps mounting up
Until I finally lose
The courage to seek its return

In some quiet
Unknown place
A piece of luggage taged with a name
Travels still
In the gloom

(Trans: John Balcom & Yingtsih Huang)

陳坤崙
Chen Kun Lun
1952～

台灣高雄人，現居高雄。《文學台灣》主力之一，主持春暉出版社與春暉印刷廠，並積極參與南台灣綠色環保運動。詩集《無言的小草》、《人間火宅》等。關注卑微人間事物，反映在作品裡的是純摯語言，以及愛和同情。

Chen Kun Lun (1952-) was born in Kaohsiung. A veteran book editor, he co-founded *Literary Taiwan* magazine in 1991, and is now director of Chuen-hwui Publishing Co. and Chuen-hwui Printing House. He has been deeply involved in green movements and ecological issues of southern Taiwan. He is author of poetry publications *Mute Little Weeds* (1974) and *Burning House of the World* (1974). His poetry of characteristic simple language expresses sympathy and love for small things of the world.

舉頭三寸

舉頭三寸
有一個神明
無時無刻在監視著你

無論你走到哪裡
他跟著你走到哪裡
你永遠無法擺脫他的跟蹤

他注意你的一舉一動
甚至你已安然睡去
他也要察看你夢裡的世界
到底隱藏著什麼

他把你的所作所為
一條不漏地記下
等你死後
做為判你下十八層地獄的證據

Three Inches above Your Head

Three inches above your head
there is a god
who watches you all the time

Wherever you go
he goes with you
you can never be rid of him

He watches your every move
even when you are asleep
he examines the hidden content
of your dream world

He writes down everything you've done
without omitting a single detail
when you die
this will be the evidence for your final judgment

(Trans: William Marr)

壺中水

裝在壺中的水
被熊熊的烈火煮著
滾過來滾過去
想逃跑
四面是堅硬的鐵牆

在壺中煮著的水
耐不住煎熬
一個一個化作青煙
飛上藍天

留在壺中的水
接受火燙身的痛苦
發出一陣又一陣的哀號
而等待喝茶解渴的
是誰啊

The Pot is Boiling

The pot is boiling
the water tries to escape
but all around there are iron walls

with burning pain
the water in the pot
finally cries out
at the tea drinker
who tries to quench his thirst

(Trans: William Marr)

掙著呼吸空氣

空間那麼大的水族館
熱帶魚
通通擠在水管的出口
掙著呼吸新鮮的空氣

Fresh Air

In a large aquarium
the tropical fish
crowd around the end of a tube
for some fresh air

(Trans: William Marr)

畫眉鳥

畫眉鳥喜歡被關在
罩著黑布的鳥籠裡

畫眉鳥
寧可生活在暗無天日的世界
也不願看到活潑聰明的人類
因為一看到眼睛閃爍不定的人
不必等到一小時
立刻驚惶而死

人到底有多可怕
至今祇有畫眉鳥知道吧

The Thrushes

The thrushes like to be shut
in bird cages cloaked in black cloth

They'd rather live in a dark world
than see a lively, smart man
for in meeting a man's quick eyes
they would fall into a panic
and soon die

Only the thrushes know
how horrible man is

(Trans: William Marr)

偷土記

住在沒有泥土的城市
僅僅為了種花
必須扮演偷土賊

拿著塑膠袋和刀子
趁著無人注意時
偷偷地下手

草和樹瞧著我
匆忙而緊張的神態
我隱約聽到

樹和風發出吱吱的笑聲
笑我是歷史上
第一個偷土的賊

A Soil Thief

In a soilless city
I have to become a soil thief
in order to cultivate flowers

When there's nobody watching
I, with a plastic bag and a knife in hand
nervously begin my stealthy act

With the grass and trees all looking at me
I seem to hear
the indistinct laughter of the wind and trees
they must be laughing at me: the first soil
thief in history

(Trans: William Marr)

利玉芳
Lih Yu Fang
1952～

台灣屏東人，現居台南，為家庭主婦及創意農牧場經營者。
詩集《活的滋味》、《貓》、《向日葵》、《夢會轉彎》等，散文集《心香瓣瓣》，兒童詩文集《我家住下營》、《小園丁》等。獨特的女性視野，在生活觀照中探觸人間性，省思社會及歷史。

Li Yu Fang (1952-) was born in Pingtung. She published her first book of essays in 1978, and began to write poems the same year. A leisure farm manager based in Tainan, she has published several poetry collections, including *The Taste of Living* (1986), *Cats* (1991), *Sunflower* (1996) and *Dreams Turn* (2010), poetry for children *The Little Gardener* (1988) and *I Live in Hsia Ying* (1999). Her works offer insights into human experience in daily life as well as reflections on history and society. She has also been dedicated to writing poems in her native Hakka language.

牛

吆喝不是我們的語言
籐條只會使我的肌肉發抖
主人啊
請用您靈犀的臂力
純熟的耕技
輕輕地牽動
繫在我鼻上的韁繩

Cows

Yelling is not language.
Rattan can only make our flesh shiver.
Oh' masters,
Please use your dexterous strength
And mature farming skills
To lead and shake lightly
The veins on my nose.

(Trans: W. H. Hsu)

鞋子

是因為你愛上了風景
我才樂意陪你去旅行

別為我專挑容易走的路
別只看我走路的姿態
別只聽我走路的聲音

但願是你走過許多風景
而不是我走過許多風景

Shoes

Because you have fallen in love with the landscape,
I am so willing to travel with you.

Don't choose the easy road because of me.
Don't just look at the posture of my walking.
Don't just listen to the sound of my walking.

I just wish that you have been to see many landscapes
And it is not I who have been to see many landscapes.

(Trans: W. H. Hsu)

向日葵

夏日的小學校園
盛開著童稚般臉蛋的向日葵
早晨
它們立正注目
東方冉冉升起的太陽
黃昏
一致向緩緩西降的落日
敬禮

規規矩矩的向日葵
是岸邊歌頌的國花
長大　才知道
意外而不敢親近
深怕中了花粉散播的毒素

現在
睜一隻眼
欣賞一簇簇金黃
長在寶島施肥的土地上
閉一隻眼
食葵花的油　嗑葵花的子
聆聽資本家為它宣傳經濟價值

喜歡
要壓低嗓子唱它的乳名──

Sunflowers

Summertime at the school yard
sunflowers bloom like innocent faces of children
in the morning
they stand to greet
the rising sun in the east
in the evening
they salute the sun
when it sets slowly in the west

The well-behaved sunflowers
which I found out when I grew up
to be the national flower on the shore
I dare not get too close
for fear of being contaminated by their poisonous pollen

Now, with one eye open
I enjoy the golden clusters
grown on the fertile soil of the island
with one eye shut
I crack and eat the roasted sunflower seeds
listen to capitalists propagandazing its
economic value

I like to
lower my voice to sing their pet names ——

日頭花日頭花滿天下愈熱它愈開花

該用什麼樣的聲音歌頌它呢？
唱——SUN FLOWER
唱——ひまわり
唱著美麗且遙遠
那…什麼事故也不會發生吧！

sunflowers sunflowers everywhere, the warmar
it gets the more
profusely they bloom

What tunes should I use to praise them?
sing—SUN FLOWERS
sing—HIMAWARI
sing the beauty and remoteness
of ... and nothing would happen!

(Trans: William Marr)

本土新書114

浮標 *Floating Beacon*

編 集 人／李敏勇 Editor / Lee Min Yung
發 行 人／魏淑貞
出 版 者／玉山社出版事業股份有限公司
　　　　　台北市106仁愛路四段145號3樓之2
　　　　　電話／（02）27753736　　傳真／（02）27753776
　　　　　電子郵件地址／ tipi395@ms19.hinet.net
　　　　　玉山社網站網址／ http://www.tipi.com.tw
　　　　　郵撥帳號／ 18599799　玉山社出版事業股份有限公司

主　　　編／蔡明雲
編　　　輯／許家旗、林邦由
行銷企畫／楊杰龍
業務行政／林志亮
法律顧問／魏千峯律師
排　　　版／極翔企業有限公司
印　　　刷／松霖彩色印刷有限公司

定　　　價／新台幣380元
初版一刷／ 2011年3月

國家圖書館出版品預行編目資料

浮標 ／李敏勇編集. -- 初版. -- 台北市：玉山
社, 2011.03
　　　面；　公分 . --（本土新書；114）

　　ISBN 978-986-6789-97-7 （平裝）

863.51　　　　　　　　　　　100001745

購買玉山社書籍的方法

◎請上玉山社網站查詢書籍（享有優惠），並直接向我們選購。
　網址：www.tipi.com.tw
　傳真電話：(02) 2775-3776
◎請向國內各大書局詢購。
◎請直接到郵局劃撥，帳號：18599799，戶名：玉山社出版事業
　（股）公司。
◎請親自到本社購買。
　地址：台北市106仁愛路四段145號3樓之2